P9-CIW-005

Everything Together

A Second Dad Wedding

Everything Together

A Second Dad Wedding

by Benjamin Klas
Illustrated by Fian Arroyo

Egremont, Massachusetts

One Elm Books is an imprint of Red Chair Press LLC
www.redchairpress.com

Free Discussion Guide available online.

Publisher's Cataloging-In-Publication Data

Names: Klas, Benjamin, author. | Arroyo, Fian, illustrator. | Klas, Benjamin. Second dad summer.

Title: Everything together / by Benjamin Klas ; illustrated by Fian Arroyo.

Description: Egremont, Massachusetts: One Elm Books, an imprint of Red Chair Press LLC, [2021] | Sequel to Second dad summer. | Interest age level: 009-013. | Summary: "When Jeremiah arrives in Minneapolis to spend the summer with his Dad, everything feels odd. His dad's fiancé, Michael, is deep into wedding plans. Jeremiah feels out of place. Never one to make new friends easily, he starts volunteering in an English class for refugees. Here, Jeremiah finds unexpected friendship. Everything Together is about exploring your place in the world and the tangled ways we connect"--Provided by publisher.

Identifiers: ISBN 9781947159655 (hardcover) | ISBN 9781947159662 (ebook)

Subjects: LCSH: Gay fathers--Juvenile fiction. | Stepfathers--Juvenile fiction. | Voluntarism--Juvenile fiction. | Friendship--Juvenile fiction. | Belonging (Social psychology)--Juvenile fiction. | CYAC: Gay fathers--Fiction. | Stepfathers--Fiction. | Voluntarism--Fiction. | Friendship--Fiction. | Belonging (Social psychology)--Fiction.

Classification: LCC PZ7.1.K635 Ev 2021 (print) | LCC PZ7.1.K635 (ebook) | DDC [Fic]--dc23

LC record available at: https://lccn.loc.gov/2020948757

Main body text set in 16/23 Sabon

Printed and bound in Canada.
0521 1P FRNF21

For Kris.
And for our neighbors from around the world
who make our country a community.

MOD
PODGE

CHAPTER

"You look like you need another coat of Mod Podge on that, Jeremiah," Michael said. "Here. Like this." He took the red punching balloon from me. It had a doily, one of those lacy circles grandmas crochet, stretched over it. He demonstrated dabbing the balloon with the gluey Mod Podge and smoothing the doily over the red surface.

"Alright," I said. "I got it." I picked up my foam brush, left long strokes of Mod Podge on the empty red space, and applied another doily. The idea was that you glued all these doilies to the punching balloon and let them dry so that when you popped the balloon, you had a lacy ball. It was kinda like paper-mache. Michael called it, “paper-ma-gay.”

He said the plan was to hang them around light bulbs in the reception hall. The pictures he showed me online were pretty impressive.

Dad and Michael were getting married the second week of August. Even though this was only the beginning of June, Michael was in full production mode, making centerpieces, wedding favors, and these lace balls.

It was my first day back visiting them for the summer, and I was already gluing doilies onto balloons. I wondered what that meant for the rest of the summer.

I stretched the next doily around the balloon, making sure the edges overlapped the last one. “Where did you get all these doilies anyway?”

Michael laughed. “Don’t ask. But really, what gay man doesn’t want a million doilies at their wedding, right?” He laughed, then stopped and looked at me seriously. “Don’t repeat that. It’s a nasty stereotype.”

“Okay,” I said. Sometimes it felt like Michael

was a collection of quite a few nasty stereotypes. But that was okay. It was what made him be him.

Michael was droning on about how hard it was to find their exact shades of teal and chocolate cloth napkins for the caterers to use. I'd learned first thing that morning that the wedding colors were teal and chocolate, not green and brown.

Halfway through my doily ball, he switched topics to RSVPs.

"You know the RSVPs were due yesterday, we've only heard from forty-two of our guests. I'm guessing about a week before the wedding we're going to get a rain of letters, people telling us they're coming. Do you know how much catering costs per plate?"

I did. He'd told me four times.

We heard heavy boots outside the apartment door. It was Dad stomping away the dirt and mud that caked onto his leather boots during the workday. He opened the door. His smell could move as fast as he could. Sweat and leather and oil. It wasn't a bad smell, but it was strong.

Dad was a major contrast to Michael. Dad was tall and thick. Michael was shorter and thin. Dad's curly brown hair stuck out from under the Timberwolves cap that always replaced his construction helmet at the end of the day. Michael's hair was straight, bleached blond, and styled so that it barely moved, even in the wind. While Dad's skin had tanned dark from his days under the sun, Michael was pale. Michael had given up tanning beds, or "fake-baking," as his New Year's resolution. Dad was bisexual. Michael was gay.

People said I looked like Dad. That we had the same dirt-brown eyes and hair. But, in my opinion, that was about where the similarities ended. Even though our hair was the same color, mine was stick straight like Mom's. I wasn't on track to be as tall as Dad, but being only 13, I hoped that could still turn around. I was starting to get some hair on my upper lip if you stared hard enough.

Dad looked from Michael, to me, to the gluey balloon. "Well, looks like you found a use for all your grandma's old doilies."

Michael laughed. "I'm sure this is what she imagined when she was crocheting them. Will you help?"

"It's what I've been training for my whole life," Dad said. "But first let me scrub off the dust."

"Be quick," Michael said. "How about you, Jeremiah? Are you up for another?"

"Uh..." I tried to look like I was really tempted by the offer. "I think I'm going outside."

"To find Sage?" Dad asked.

"Hopefully," I said.

"Oh, that reminds me," Michael said. He stood up, and started rummaging through a pile of papers on the hutch. "I know it's around here somewhere. This. No. Aha. Here." He held an envelope out to me.

I took it. Three names in calligraphy: Sage, Reina, & Lisa. Sage was my best friend from last summer. Reina and Lisa were her moms. "I can invite them?"

"Of course," Michael said. "But make sure they know to RSVP ASAP."

"Thanks," I said, pulling on my sneakers.

"Tell Sage *Hi*," Dad said. "Ask her to save you from Michael's Pinterest projects."

"Ha ha," Michael said, then started blowing up another balloon.

"This summer, maybe the two of you will explore the other half of Minneapolis," Dad said.

Michael tied off the balloon. "Or the rest of Minnesota."

"You could start a new community garden." Dad said.

"Or save another old man in need," Michael said.

"Or just save the rest of the neighborhood," Dad said.

"Or—"

"Geez," I interrupted them. That's what life was like with Sage. Open. Alive. But I snorted and held up the invitation. "I just have to deliver this."

I walked down the three flights of steps and out the front door. The sun was bright. The wind blew until the trees danced in the park across the street. The park is where we always met up last year.

And there she was, across the street lying on her back on the green grass of the park. Her giant curly mass of hair made a pillow under and around her head. The light glittered off her rainbow sequin sundress as she stared up into the sky with those wide green eyes. She had often done this last summer, lying back, naming the clouds that floated by as if they were a family. Same place, same Sage.

Making friends was never easy for me, but somehow with Sage our friendship practically grew by itself. She had two moms like I was about to have two dads. The Stevens Square neighborhood was full of what Dad and Michael called "DINKs" (double income, no kids), which meant that finding another person my age had felt super lucky. She was alone. I was alone. Maybe when there aren't a whole lot of other options, it's easier to be friends with whoever comes your way.

Even though she was the only option, I still really liked her. I never knew what kind of things might happen when she was around, whether that was going to be an epic bike ride along the Mississippi, or searching for her favorite paintings at the art museum.

I smiled as I started across the street. It was only then that I noticed someone was lying next to Sage.

Another girl her age.

She wasn't alone anymore.

I was.

CHAPTER

There were many problems with the whole *staying with Dad for the summer* thing. I loved it and all but it was also hard to switch back and forth between Iowa and the Twin Cities. Leaving all my friends for three months always made me the outsider when I returned in time for school. Sure, I could text them and

I did. But mostly, texting them just showed me over and over what I was missing with them. Three months was just enough time to be out of the loop about everything.

And then coming to stay with Dad and Michael, I had been away from them for nine months and had to catch up. I had to hope that whatever friends I'd made the previous summer were still going to be my friends this year. Sage and I only had last summer together, but still, she was my best friend in Minneapolis.

But now there was this stranger. The girl lying next to Sage seemed to share her love of bright colors. Her long skirt was hot pink, and her dark brown face and shoulders were surrounded by a purple head-covering with crystals sewn on. It was a hijab. Michael had taught me the word. A lot of the women and girls I saw at the library wore them. It was a pretty common thing for Muslim women to wear.

I thought about turning around, going back inside before Sage could notice me. Instead, I took a deep breath and stood on the stoop like I had so many mornings last summer. I was trying to buy time to decide what to do.

I looked over the flower beds on either side of the apartment steps. Last summer, the garden only had a few ratty *potentilla fruticosa* bushes surrounded by landscape rocks. Sage and I spent hours clearing away rocks so daylilies could join the bushes. Daylilies were Mr. Keeler's favorite, but he was gone now. He had a stroke last July and died. Now it was just me and the garden.

I folded Sage's wedding invitation in half, slid it into my back pocket, and turned back towards the door.

"Jeremiah?" It was Sage's voice: bright and light, even though it was yelled across the street.

I turned around. Sage sat up now, and so did the other girl. When Sage saw my face, she shrieked. She ran towards me, her arms held over her head. She bounded across the street and threw her arms around me. We hadn't hugged before, so this was kind of new. Several twigs and leaves stuck out of her bushy black hair, probably from lying on the ground. Her green eyes were huge and twinkling.

"I've been waiting for a million years for you to finally get back. When did you get here? You never texted me when you'd get here. Wait. Maybe you did, and I just forgot."

I couldn't help but smile. I was being stupid. Worrying about nothing. "Last night," I said.

"Okay," Sage said, grabbing my hand. "Come on. Come on."

She pulled me towards the park where the other girl sat up, watching us with a big smile. She didn't seem surprised to see me. She adjusted her hijab and bounded over to us. The new girl was taller than Sage.

"Jeremiah, I would like you to meet the exuberant, benevolent, and magnificent Asha!"

Asha giggled. "You forgot harmonious."

Sage's voice deepened and she put on an intense expression like she was an announcer at a sports event. "Let's give it up for the exuberant, benevolent, magnificent, and nearly always harmonious, Asha!"

Asha bowed. I clapped a few times because it seemed like what they were going for. This was a bit much. Sage was a lot to handle, even when she was on her own. Apparently, she was a lot more with Asha.

"She's pretty much my other half now," Sage said, swinging her arm around Asha. "Twins."

"Twins?" I said.

Sage laughed. "We do everything together."

Everything? I hadn't considered that I could have been replaced.

"Sage talks about you a lot," Asha said, which made me feel just a little bit better. "I'll bet I know what's coming next."

Sage looked at her. "A bike ride?" She looked at me. "I told her it's kinda our thing," Sage mumbled.

Our thing. That was something. I nodded, making myself smile. "I'll go upstairs and get my helmet."

Our thing. I was getting worried over nothing. Sage hadn't replaced me. It was going to be fine.

When I told Michael where I was off to, he smiled. "Reconnecting with your bestie," he said.

"Have fun," Dad said.

Michael pointed at me. "And watch out—"

"For potholes," Dad and I finished for him.

I didn't mention Asha.

I went to the cool, dimly lit basement where everyone in the building locked their bikes. I wiped nine months of dust off my bike, pumped the tires, and hauled it outside.

Sage and Asha waited in front of my building with their bikes. Sage's bike was magenta. Asha's was pale pink.

Asha hiked up her skirt and I saw that she was wearing skinny jeans underneath it. She got onto her bike. "I had to reclaim it from my brother," she said. "Even though it's mine, I've been sharing. His was stolen."

"See?" said Sage. "I told you she was benevolent."

When I sat on my bike, I noticed it was too small for me. I grew a lot since last summer. I probably looked ridiculous.

I kicked up the kickstand. "Where should we go?"

"Let's go to—" Sage started.

"Thomas Lowry." Asha finished.

"Totally," Sage said. She turned to me. "We found a new park by the sculpture gardens. It has a river through it. Just a fake one, but still."

"Sure," I said, and we were off.

As we pedaled, I found that there was never enough room for three cyclists to ride side by side. I was always trailing behind as Sage and Asha pedaled forward. I watched them, turning their heads towards each other, exchanging words I was too far back to hear. The only sound I could understand from them was their laughter.

I was relieved when we pulled off the sidewalk towards the sound of rushing water and towards the shade of a big oak tree. Thomas Lowry Park was kind of cool if you could get past the fact that the water feature taking up the whole park was artificial. Sage and Asha ripped off their shoes and waded into the water. I sat in the grass, not quite sure if I was ready to jump in with both feet.

I stared up at the sky. Cumulonimbus clouds towered in the blue. "Hey Sage," I called over the sound of the running water. "What do you think about that one?"

"That what?" Sage asked.

"The cloud. What's its name?"

"Oh yeah," Sage said with a laugh. "I used to name clouds. I kinda forgot."

"You're so fabulous," Asha said.

I watched as they started kicking water at each other, laughing and shrieking.

I could tell right then that everything was going to be different this summer. When they started kicking water at me, I told them to stop. I got up and moved further away to where their laughter wouldn't be able to splash over me.

CHAPTER 3

Michael was making Dad and I memorize his family tree. Michael kept flipping through a photo album and showing us the faces that went with each name. He'd started with his parents and "baby sisters" who were twenty-eight and thirty. Then we'd moved on to parents, aunts, uncles, cousins. It was surprising how big his family was.

"This is my great Aunt Aggie," he said, pointing to a face that looked like a wrinkled apple.

"Cute," I said. Which she actually was, in a wrinkled apple kind of way.

"I can see the resemblance," Dad said.

"Shut up," Michael laughed. "But she's not even going to be at the wedding. So, you can forget her face."

"Already forgotten," Dad said.

Michael turned the page. "Um… Oh! This is my cousin Ted. He might make it. He's a geologist." The man looked like a short, thick version of Indiana Jones. "And Juniper, who is non-binary. My Aunt Maja from Poland. My other cousin Ted who runs marathons."

Michael went on and on.

By the time he'd moved into his second cousin who was an accountant and her ex-husband who was a "wretched-rotten-filthy-liar," I was officially ready to never look at another photo ever again.

I stole a look out the window for some sign of Sage or Asha. I still felt weird about the ride yesterday. There was nothing wrong with Asha. She was fun and friendly. She sparkled.

I definitely did not.

Why hadn't Sage mentioned her in any texts or emails? Not that there were all that many, but still. I tried to review them in my mind. Maybe she had mentioned a new friend. Maybe I assumed it was just another person from school, not someone from the neighborhood.

It wasn't hard to spot them because the two of them glittered in the sun. Asha was apparently trying to teach Sage to do a cartwheel. Asha could do them with impressive skill. Each time she turned upside down, the legs of her jeans stuck out from the blossom of her dress. Every time Sage tried one, she launched herself forward only to fall flat after doing a half handstand.

Finally, they collapsed in a pile, laughing together. Truth be told, I didn't like to share, not parents, not friends. I know that sounds selfish, but being one person's friend was hard enough without trying to be friends with several of them.

"Would you look at that!" Dad's voice snapped me back to the mounds and layers of photos. Maybe we would need Michael's geologist cousin to excavate us. Dad was holding a photo out to me. A kid probably around my age was standing on a soccer field in uniform with a ball tucked under his arm. He scowled at the camera.

"Wait," I said, recognizing the face. "You played soccer?" I asked Michael.

Michael took the photo back and studied it. "From sixth grade all the way through twelfth."

"Wow." Somehow I hadn't pictured him as the sports type.

He started digging through a box of photos. "I think I've got the photo of my senior team. Somewhere... In here..."

I tried to signal Dad with my eyes, sending him an S.O.S. He got the message.

"Alright," Dad said. "I think that's all the

photos I'll be able to remember."

Michael stopped searching. "I just have another two boxes."

"Sir," Dad said in his deep voice, "I am going to have to ask you to put down the photos and step away with your hands up. I repeat, put down the albums."

Michael sighed, then looked at the clock. "How were we doing that for over an hour? Time flies when you're having fun, doesn't it?" He looked at me.

"Um," I said. "I plead the fifth. I have the right to remain silent."

Dad laughed, so did Michael.

"Fine," Michael said, sweeping the piles of photographs back into stacks and closing up the albums. "We'll come back to it. I've got work to do on those jars anyways."

He and Dad got up and started unloading several cases of empty canning jars onto the dining room table.

I picked up my phone and checked for

anything. My phone was ancient. It was one of those ones that flipped open and only really worked for calls, texts, and the world's blurriest pictures. I'd gotten a text from Terrell, my friend back home.

just won madden with the vikings. hope MN is fun

I texted back, *so far so good*. I was trying to be optimistic.

I thought about texting Sage, but I looked out the window at her and Asha, and decided not to.

I joined Dad and Michael. Michael pulled on a pair of latex gloves and squirted a type of clear paint into a used yogurt container. He picked up the first canning jar.

"You remind me of Mom," I said. "She has about this many jars in canning season." But I knew these weren't for salsa.

"I don't envy her," Michael said, dabbing the jar with a foam brush. He coated the inside of the jar until it had an even teal tint. "I've got more of these brushes if you want to make yourself useful."

Dad laughed. "There is nothing I'd rather do," he said sitting down and squirting himself a cup of paint. He skipped the gloves and started dabbing away, leaving long, streaky stripes. Michael looked like he was trying to pin his lips together and not comment on Dad's contribution.

"Well?" Michael finally opened his mouth and was staring at me. "Are you going to help? If not, you shouldn't be standing in these paint fumes."

"And you should be?" I asked.

He laughed, a sort of nervous, crazy laugh. "I'm not worried about fumes. If I have any brains or sanity left at all after the wedding, it will be a miracle."

As my good action for the day, I found a box fan and put it in the window to increase the ventilation. "For your sanity," I said.

For something to do, I went downstairs to see if the mail had come. At the front door, I looked out at Sage and Asha. I almost went out to join them, but something held me back.

I turned away and retrieved the mail and brought it upstairs.

"Two more RSVPs," I said, recognizing the shape and size of the envelopes.

Michael took off his gloves and took the mail from me. He opened them quickly and scanned one, then the other. He closed each of them back into their envelopes like they were something indecent.

"Well?" Dad looked up from another streaky jar.

"Your parents." Michael paused. "And your sister."

Dad gave a laugh that showed nothing about this was funny to him. "All the good news in one day, huh? And?"

"Do you really want to know?" Michael asked.

"No," Dad said. "But show me anyways."

Michael pulled them back out of their envelopes and handed them to Dad.

I thought I had an idea what might've been

on that RSVP. When Dad had married Mom, his parents thought he was 'healed' from being bisexual like it was a disease or something. They thought Dad shouldn't marry another man.

"About what I expected from my parents," Dad said. "But Paula said she might come. That's more than I expected."

Michael snorted. "Perfect. So, I get to have more unknowns for the caterers. Paula's whole family is nine spots!" Michael breathed out through his teeth. "Sorry. This isn't about a seating chart. It's about you. And them. And their list of scripture verses."

Dad pulled Michael into a hug. "They have their own baggage. All we can do is love them on their journey."

"Love them on their journey?" I said. "That sounds like something Pastor Veronica would say."

Dad laughed. "Yeah, I might've stolen it from her."

"Well," Michael said. "You have more charity

in your heart than I do. I think they suck."

"How did I land a guy like you?" Dad kissed Michael.

"Gross," I said.

"We will have none of your homophobia, young man," Michael said with a grin.

I stuck out my tongue.

We all laughed.

Dad sat down and picked up his brush again. As he painted the inside of another jar, his mouth was pulled into a smile, but his eyes weren't. His eyes looked like he was in pain.

CHAPTER

This first week back wasn't going like I'd planned. Instead of going off on adventures with Sage like we did last summer, I spent days tagging along with whatever Sage and Asha were already doing.

By the time Thursday rolled around, I wasn't surprised to step out of the apartment to find

Sage and Asha practicing double somersaults. I made myself cross the street to the park to join them, but I had never even been able to do a single somersault. I just sat and watched.

"Watch this!" Sage commanded before running halfway down the little hill in the park. She picked up enough momentum to launch herself into a forward flip. She landed with both feet on the ground, but her body kept moving and she wiped out.

"Holy crap," I said. "Are you okay?"

She stood up, wiping strands of embedded grass from her hands and forehead. She and Asha were laughing.

"Well," Sage said. "Maybe you should've stopped watching before the end there."

"Since when do you know how to do flips?" I asked, but I knew the answer.

"Asha," Sage said. Asha gave a ceremonious bow. "She's in gymnastics and tumbling and we're thinking about becoming hardcore parkour sensations on YouTube."

Asha sighed. "But my parents don't want me posting videos of myself online."

"What about your parents?" I asked Sage.

Sage gave me one of her airiest smiles. "I haven't gotten around to mentioning it to them."

After watching another dozen or so attempts, I asked, "Isn't there anything else you two do?" It didn't come out particularly nicely.

Sage didn't seem to notice my tone of voice, though. "We're starting a band."

"A band?" I asked.

Asha nodded, then started doing air guitar. "I'm learning electric guitar," she said. "I'm really starting to shred."

"I'm on drums," Sage said. "You should join!"

Was there anything they did that I could be a part of? Besides the bike rides that practically crowded me out? The only instrument I had ever played was the violin when I was in second and third grade. Mom made me stop because she said the screeching gave her migraines, and I had agreed happily.

"We could do band practice this afternoon!" Asha said.

Sage agreed, then turned to me. "Wanna get on the bandwagon?"

I shrugged. "Probably not. I've got some reading to catch up on," I said. I thought it sounded like a good excuse.

And I did have some reading. Last summer I tackled *The Grapes of Wrath*. This year, Mom had finally made me a list of novels that weren't written by "dead white dudes." I'd picked *A Tree Grows in Brooklyn*. So far it was about a girl, Francie, who basically lived off her imagination and books in the middle of her family's fight to get enough to eat and pay rent.

I didn't want to be part of their band, but at the same time, a tiny part of me wanted them to insist I join them, or at least attend practice.

But they didn't. Sage said, "Suit yourself," and watched as Asha demonstrated another perfect double somersault.

By the time I'd gone back to the apartment, I

was starting to feel hollow.

My phone buzzed. A message from Terrell.

beach day

There was also a picture which my phone's ancient abilities couldn't open.

Looks fun.

Even though I couldn't see the picture, I knew it had to be more fun than I was having at the moment.

That night after supper, Michael made Dad change into something "cuter."

"You can't go to Cocktail Hour in a tank and cut-offs," Michael said.

Cocktail Hour was something Dad and Michael did every week. They got together with a group of friends at someone's apartment to have a drink and talk about articles they'd read, the news, and generally about their lives.

Dad went to the bedroom and came out a few minutes later wearing a brown patterned dress shirt.

Michael shook his head. "Brown?"

"Not brown," Dad said. "Chocolate."

All of us laughed.

"Touché," Michael said. "Wanna come, Jer?"

I thought about it for a minute, then said, "Yeah. I think I will."

Dad and Michael both looked surprised. I wondered if they had only asked me as a formality. Last year, they'd invited me to cocktail hour every week, but I'd only accepted once.

"Great," Dad said. And from his smile, I thought he was actually happy I was coming along.

"We'll ride," Michael said. "Robi and Em live in Lyndale. Near Uptown." That was just a fifteen-minute ride away.

We hauled our bikes up from the basement. Michael went first, with the Uni-cycle, his bike that he decorated to look like a unicorn, complete with a plush unicorn head, rainbow streamers, and a frame coated in glitter. Last summer, I had been super embarrassed any time

I had to be in public with it.

By this summer, I had come to accept that it was just Michael. And people who stared were really staring at him, not me.

Outside, we buckled on our helmets.

As we rolled down the alley, Michael called out, "Watch out for potholes!"

"I know," I said. And I did. I'd had a nasty blowout last summer. But as I rolled down the alley, I wasn't watching for potholes; I was watching between buildings for glimpses of the park. I couldn't help it. It wasn't until the last gap that I saw what I'd been watching for.

Sage.

She was sitting in front of Asha. Asha was compressing Sage's hair into French braids.

"Jer!" Dad yelled from behind me. I slammed on my brakes right before running into Michael who had stopped at the end of the alley to look both ways.

It was close, but no crash. Still, I could feel my cheeks go red. "Sorry."

Dad rolled to a stop behind me. "What were you looking at, Jeremiah?"

I shook my head. "Nothing," I said. But really, it felt like a whole lot. "I just want to get to cocktail hour." That part was true.

Did I say that riding with Michael on the Unicycle wasn't embarrassing anymore? I take that back. While we rode, people catcalled and yelled to Michael who gave them that kind of wave royalty did in parades.

Michael was Michael. But holy crap, he could still be embarrassing.

Em and Robi lived on the second floor of an old brick house. We locked our bikes against the fence and walked up the wide wooden steps.

Em greeted us at the door. She had short blond hair, and her arms and neck were covered in star tattoos that spread from the sleeves and neck of her Wonder Woman t-shirt. The logo was in the light blue, white, and pink of the trans flag. I'd forgotten she was trans.

"Jeremiah! It's been forever!" she said, waving us through the doorway into a small, bright kitchen.

"10 months," I said. Em, Dad and Michael laughed.

Em's partner, Robi, crowded into the room with us. Robi pulled Michael into a hug, then they slapped Dad on the shoulder, and held out their fist to me for a fist bump. Robi was gender queer, and they were the first person I'd met who didn't go by *he* or *she*, but used *they* and *them* instead. They wore a pair of Carhartt overalls over a rose-printed tank top.

"I like your beard," I said to Robi. Last year their beard had been thin and wispy. This year, it was a lot thicker, and long enough to pull the hair under their chin into a short braid.

"Thank you, sir," they said, giving the braid a tug.

Em led us into the living room while Robi got us drinks. The rest of the guests were perched on stools or sunk into the low couch and chairs.

They called out welcomes to me and all wanted to shake my hand or give me a hug.

I tried to remember all their names. Mary from Canada and her wife Josephina from Columbia. Sarah, with the beaded dreadlocks that hung down past her waist. Heather and Dave with their baby, Gordon, who was now crawling around with a green rubber frog hanging from his mouth like a dog with a bone. Short, pudgy, and blond Jon and his partner Ben, who was tall and thin with speckled white hair that was bright against his dark brown skin. They referred to themselves as Big Ben and Little Jon, like the clock in London and Robin Hood's faithful companion.

I picked my way through the minefield of baby toys to an empty chair between Sarah and Michael.

Robi brought our drinks: a beer for Dad, a gin and tonic for Michael, and a tonic with lime for me. "It was either this or water for minors such as yourself," Robi laughed, handing me my drink. It was tart and bitter—very different as far as soda-type things went. I liked it.

Before they started talking about the current events, the group focused on me. They asked how my school year had been. Whether I was still taking care of the garden in front of the building. How many Pinterest projects Michael had roped me into.

"And how about your friend?" Robi asked. "What was her name? Parsley, Sage, Rosemary or Thyme?"

Everyone laughed except for me. "Sage," I said. I didn't know how to respond. I didn't really want to talk about it. "Her name is Sage." I left it at that and nobody pressed.

The conversation moved on to the upcoming elections. Which candidates were going to support rights and equality for LGBTQ people. But not just that community. They talked a lot about rights for refugees and undocumented people.

"And people keep calling them things like,

'illegal aliens,'" Sarah said. "Just another way to distance 'them' from 'us.'"

Em said, "Some people are afraid of refugees. But look at Minneapolis. We've got so many refugees here, and what kind of scary things do they do? Start small businesses?"

"Right?" Robi said. "I wish anyone who had talked crap about refugees would come and visit the school where I volunteer. Let them at least know the faces and stories of these amazing people they are trashing."

They talked about the protest that had happened last week at the capitol and about the upcoming pride festival.

I sipped my tonic and mostly just listened. They talked about all sorts of things that I didn't know enough about to really join in, but it was interesting all the same.

When baby Gordon got tired of chewing all of his toys and leaving little puddles of drool, Heather and Dave said they needed to go get him to bed. It wasn't even 7:00.

"Life is different with a kid," Dave said while they collected the explosion of toys back into their diaper bag. "You lose a lot of freedom."

I looked guiltily from Dad to Michael.

"You trade in one great life for another," Dad said, which made me feel a little better.

Heather beamed. "And I wouldn't take it back for anything."

When they left, the conversation switched to lighter things. And like all things with Michael these days, they switched to the wedding.

"Of course, it is going to be an outdoor wedding," he said.

"In August?" Sarah said. "Fine. I guess I'll live!"

"It has to be outdoors," Michael said. "Everyone in my family gets married outside, next to the water, under the open sky. It's tradition. My grandparents got married next to a cow pond on their farm. My parents married on the shore of Lake Superior. My sister got married on the banks of the Saint Croix. Allen and I will get married on the shores of Powderhorn Lake. We rented the pavilion for the reception."

I went to Powderhorn last year. It was a park a few miles from our apartment with a lake sunk in the middle. It would make a nice place for a wedding.

"It's a step up from Lake Superior," Dad said with a laugh. "And after we say our vows, I'm gonna throw Michael in the lake."

"Ha ha," Michael said, then started his spiel about the drama of caterers, the pile of unfinished DIY projects, and unanswered RSVPs.

I didn't care whether they got married inside or outside or upside down. Between all the obsession with the wedding and Sage ignoring me, I was almost ready for this summer to be done.

CHAPTER

Saturday morning I ducked out of an invitation from Dad and Michael to go pick up tiny picture frames for nameplates at the craft store.

"Are you sure?" Dad asked. "It's the craft store. It's always full of wonder." He said it dryly, giving Michael a little punch.

"Wonder and majesty," Michael said.

"I'll pass," I said. "I'm gonna hang out with Sage today." I hadn't actually made any plans with her, but she was usually around on a Saturday.

"Back with your bestie," Michael said. *Bestie.* That was, apparently, his new favorite word.

I nodded. "Yeah." I hoped that was true.

When they left, I texted Sage. *Wanna hang out?*

As I waited for a reply I locked the apartment behind me and went down to the stoop. Last summer, I had thought of it as Mr. Keeler's stoop. He was always smoking cigarettes there. This summer, I was already starting to think of it as my stoop. Not that nobody else in the building used it, and it offered a great vantage point to the park and let me look at the gardens.

The dead petunias still surrounded the daylilies. I needed to do something about it. I knew that. But somehow it was harder to work on the garden this year. Harder without the motivation of making it for Mr. Keeler.

My phone buzzed. *Mom is taking us to MOA. Wanna come?*

MOA. The Mall of America. I hadn't been there before, but I knew it was a giant mall south of Minneapolis.

I texted Dad and got the okay.

Yep, I texted back to Sage.

I grabbed the wedding invitation, then went outside to meet up with Sage and one of her moms, Lisa. Lisa was Sage's Hmong mom. She had short, spiky black hair and a smile that nearly split her face in half. She wore khaki shorts and a navy blue t-shirt that said SECRETLY LESBIAN on it. Sage, meanwhile, wore a breezy sundress covered in neon butterflies.

"Morning, Jeremiah," Lisa said.

"Hi, Lisa." It was always weird calling her Lisa to her face. Back home, I was used to calling adults Mr. this or Mrs. that. But everyone here seemed to go on a first-name basis.

She said we were going to take the light rail to the mall. It was like a subway but didn't go underground much. Michael liked to call it the "aboveway." But instead of going to the bus that took us downtown to the light rail, I followed them to another apartment. It was another older brick building, half-covered in Virginia Creeper vines.

A girl sat on the stoop.

Asha.

Apparently the "us" Sage was talking about in her text was Sage and Asha. My heart sank a little. It was gonna be another day of being the outsider, the third wheel.

I slid the invitation into my pocket, wondering whether I'd ever get to deliver it.

Asha sat on the front steps of her apartment building talking to a boy who sat on a parked bicycle. He looked like he was probably around her age, about the same height, and his face was the same dark brown.

When we were half a block away, Asha saw

us, squealed, and ran over. The boy smiled and waved. I lifted my hand, wondering if he was coming, too, and there would be *two* new people for me to try to figure out. My sinking heart started tightening up, but I had nothing to worry about. He rode the other way.

"Asha's brother," Sage explained as I watched him. Honestly, I was relieved when he turned his handlebars and disappeared around the corner. I thought the day would be complicated enough as a third wheel and not a fourth.

"Hellooo!" Asha said. She wore a long dress with sleeves that went down to her wrist with a large, glittery butterfly on the front.

"We coordinated," Sage told me as she pulled Asha into a side hug that turned into them walking side by side, arms around each other's shoulders.

"You should've warned me," I said, and made myself smile. "I could've worn my butterfly leggings."

Everyone laughed.

I looked at Sage and Asha who were already talking with their heads together.

Third wheel.

No. I wasn't the third wheel.

It was fine.

As we walked it didn't take long to realize that, just like riding bikes, walking three side by side was always just a little too big for the sidewalks. I kept having to fall back a step to get around sign posts or fire hydrants. But they didn't mean anything by it.

It was fine.

By the time we got on the bus to connect to the light rail, I was determined to keep stepping up to keep the row of three going. On the bus, though, and on the light rail, the seats came in sets of two, so I had to sit with Lisa while Sage and Asha chattered away about who knows what.

"How's your summer been?" Lisa asked.

"All seven days of it?" I asked.

Lisa laughed. I looked across the aisle to Sage

and Asha. Sage's head was tilted back in a laugh at whatever it was that Asha had just said.

I sighed. "It's fine."

"Lots of wedding preparations?" she asked.

I rolled my eyes. "You have no idea."

Talking with Lisa turned out to be okay. She was interesting. We talked about what kind of music we liked. She asked what books I was reading these days. Apparently, she'd also read *A Tree Grows in Brooklyn* and it was one of her favorites. She said that there weren't many books about Hmong kids in Minnesota, so a book about white immigrants in Brooklyn was about as close as she could get to a really relatable story when she was growing up.

Talking to Lisa wasn't like talking to a friend, necessarily, but it was nice. I was thankful to have the full attention of someone who wasn't distracted by a pile of wedding decorations or their new *bestie*.

Finally, we got off the light rail. The Mall of America was impressive. Four storeys. The stores formed in a giant circle around an indoor theme park with roller coasters, a carousel, and a Ferris wheel. Every square inch of the place was selling something.

Just like at the library, Sage led us on a meandering path. I hadn't really considered how shopping with Sage might look. But of course, it involved going into a lot of stores that were very pink and glittery.

But we went to other places, too. Like a bead store. And a tiny store that sold nothing but lucky bamboo. We got a giant bag of jalapeño cheddar popcorn to share. We went into board game stores and the Lego store with Lego creations that reached into the second and third floor.

Lisa lagged behind as Sage led Asha and me through the crowded mall. I did my best to stay next to Sage as if being close could somehow confirm our friendship, but I found out that mall walking as the extra friend was its own kind of parkour. Too bad it would make a lousy

YouTube channel. By the time we passed the roller coaster, I'd dodged three pillars, seven garbage cans, and had gotten stuck behind two women in matching tracksuits for several minutes before Sage and Asha noticed and waited up.

I looked for things to connect me to Sage and break through her endless conversational flow with Asha. At a no-smoking sign near the restrooms I reminded Sage of Mr. Keeler and how he used to throw his cigarette butts everywhere.

Sage and Asha wanted to stop into a music store to look at electric guitars. They talked more about the band they wanted to start and what to name it.

I pointed out a unicorn hat in the window of a shop and reminded Sage about when we had to take the Uni-cycle to Uptown last summer.

Asha pulled Sage into an earring store and found a pair of blue heart studs that Sage decided she just had to buy.

“Don’t these remind you of—” Asha said.

“Yes!” Sage said.

I searched the store for something else. Something to connect us. I finally settled on a pair of earrings with enamel clouds that dangled from the ends. “What do you think these clouds are named?” I asked.

“Tiny and Burt,” Sage laughed, which was something.

Sage pulled Asha over to a kiosk and they bought matching turquoise and lavender wrist bands.

I found a mini-donut stand and bought a bag to share with Sage. Of course I shared with Asha, too. But I knew they were Sage’s favorite.

Back and forth. Back and forth.

It seemed like Sage didn’t even notice. Maybe you don’t have to notice stuff like that when you’re the one in the middle everyone is pulling on.

The worst part, though, was when I realized that Asha wasn’t pulling. She just knew that

Sage would swing back. When you're not afraid of losing anything, you don't have to grip it so tight. No matter how I pulled, the two of them just snapped back together like magnets.

By the time that Lisa led us to a food court for lunch, I was ready to sit down and have something else to do besides keep fighting for Sage.

"What do you think of the mall?" Sage asked me. "The capitol of capitalism!"

I shrugged. "It's fine."

Sage raised her eyebrows.

"Good," I said. "It's good." Which wasn't a lie. The mall itself had been interesting. The Lego and board game store were exciting enough. And I could see that we weren't far from a bookstore up ahead. After lunch, though, we didn't make it to the bookstore without another detour.

"Build-a-Bear next!" Asha said.

As they went through the store hugging furry animals, I tried to find something in the store to connect to a memory of last summer.

Asha and Sage squealed over a bear passport, or "Paws-port."

I scanned the shelves for something. Anything.

But there was nothing.

I didn't even try to find anything for the rest of our trip.

When I finally got home, Dad and Michael were sitting at the table. Dad was peeling price tags off the backs of the mountain of mini picture frames. Michael opened each one to remove the black and white example pic, then carefully closed them up again.

"How was the mall?" Dad asked.

I took a deep breath and pulled a smile across my face. "It was fine."

I went to my room, dug the rumpled invitation from my pocket, and buried it in the bottom of my sock drawer.

CHAPTER

"What kind of crazy garden shenanigans are you up to this summer?" Mom asked during one of her phone call check-ups. "Are the—what were they again? Tiger lilies? The ones you planted last year? Are they blooming?"

"Daylilies," I said.

"Yeah, those," she continued. "Have they

returned with a vengeance?"

I was sitting on the stoop, so I had a prime view of the lilies. Their thick grassy foliage was a vibrant green. Already, they were pushing buds up towards the sun. "With a vengeance," I said. "How are the tomatoes?"

She just laughed. After the success of her tomato patch last year, she said she had resigned. She wanted to end her gardening career on a good note. As opposed to the note of killing everything that she had tried to grow all the years before. "You know what I am thinking about growing? Topiary. Those tiny trees. I think it might be easier to remember to take care of them since they grow inside. I could put one on the windowsill next to my easel."

"Do you mean bonsai?" I asked.

She laughed. "Yep, those."

I couldn't picture her working with something as finicky as a bonsai that had to be trained and trimmed and all that.

"How are those boring old fogies treating

you?" Mom asked. I was thankful for the change of subject so I didn't have to warn her about the temperament of bonsai.

"Okay," I said. "Dad is working long days, but we get to go for rides and hang out at night while Michael is working his night shifts at Real Foods."

"Still into that, is he?" Mom asked.

"It's his job."

I could almost see her shaking her head. "Real Foods. As if what the rest of us eat isn't real." Mom didn't have a high opinion of organic food. The way she saw it, organic was just another way for corporate farming to charge us more. "At least it's better than the Pop Tarts® and Hot Pockets® your father used to feed you all summer."

To be honest, I didn't mind that diet too much either. But I was starting to like Michael's cooking. You never knew what to expect.

"I'm gonna go," I said. "Maybe I'll work on the garden some."

"Love and kisses, Jer Bear!"

When I hung up, I took one last look at the garden, then went back inside.

I hoped my second week in Minneapolis would be better than my first.

Monday, I texted Sage. She said she was in the middle of parkour practice, and did I want to learn how to leapfrog dumpsters?

I didn't.

Instead I got to spend the morning finishing the painted canning jars.

I texted Sage Tuesday. She and Asha were hooking up the new amp for the electric guitar and did I want to join them?

I didn't.

Instead I got to stain the wooden napkin rings with acrylic stain. 50 in teal. 50 in chocolate.

Wednesday, I didn't text at all. I thought it was Sage's turn. I kept the phone close by while I assembled a series of multi-tiered "canapé" trays. I didn't dare risk a 40-minute lesson by asking what a canapé was.

Sage never texted.

Days rolled by. I picked a spot near the window so I could watch for Sage in the park. But she always had Asha. Never once did she look up towards my window. Part of me knew I should just go down and try a handstand or something. But the other part of me stubbornly waited for Sage to invite me, even if I didn't want to do what they were doing.

I often found myself straying back to the window overlooking the park. I was drawn to it like a tongue is drawn to the gap in your mouth when you lose a tooth. Every time I saw them I felt something heavy in my stomach.

I was getting tired of the mornings filled with Mod Podge, scrapbook paper, canning jars, paint, and Michael. I started going for bike rides by myself. When I went outside, I took my bike out the back door and rode around the places Sage and I had used to explore. Down to the Stone Arch Bridge. The Franklin Library. The

Minneapolis Institute of the Arts.

Halfway through the morning, when I got tired of checking my phone, I sat down to help Michael make wedding favors.

"Soap," said Michael. "I don't know how many times I've come away from a wedding with some kind of memento that I had no use for. Like once, the two brides had 'unity sand' that they poured together, blue and red, instead of a unity candle. And we all came away from the wedding with a tiny vial of purple sand. What the heck am I supposed to do with that?"

"So, soap?" I said. "Isn't that kinda weird, too? Thanks for coming to the wedding. Now go wash yourself up." I knew immediately that I shouldn't have said anything. It was best not to challenge Michael about anything wedding related. He had a pretty short fuse these days.

Michael set his lips firmly together and laid out the supplies. "Soap. It will be cute and useful and it's too late to turn back now."

We melted down big bars of glycerin soap and

mixed in a combination of cocoa powder and coffee grounds. We poured it into little square silicone molds.

"Cocoa powder helps renew and firm your skin," Michael said. "And the coffee grounds are exfoliating. Plus, chocolate brown."

The soap smelled good. Like mocha. I wasn't sure that I would like to lather mocha all over my body, but to each their own.

Then it was a batch of teal glycerin mixed with eucalyptus oil, also a good smell. Bright and sharp. It was a better soap smell in my opinion.

In the end we had almost two hundred tiny soaps in the wedding colors.

We stacked them, one of each color, alternating between brown on top and teal on top. Michael had me measure and cut lengths of white ribbon to tie each stack. He even had a special way we were supposed to tie the bows so they turned out even each time.

"Well, that's enough for one day," Michael

said, surveying the piles of soaps and the two dozen or so tied soap bundles. “I need some fresh air. And quinoa. Come to Real Foods with me?”

“I’ve got plans,” I said. It had been my excuse most afternoons after a morning of wedding DIY wonder. Of course, I didn’t have plans. Unless you count wandering around aimlessly until you take a bike ride then come home to try to read a novel.

Michael grabbed his canvas NPR bag. “You have fun. Give my best to Sage.”

I nodded.

When Michael left, I walked around the apartment. I looked out the windows at the park. I was starting to feel a little bit like some kind of spy or creeper. So I picked up my phone instead. I pretended I was going to text Sage, but when I opened the text and saw the last one about the Mall of America, I flipped my phone shut.

Dad came home before Michael got back. I

heard him stomping the dirt off his boots on the rug outside the apartment. He brought in his smell of earth, leather, oil and sweat. I was sitting at the table practicing tying the perfect ribbon bow, trying to ignore the sounds of Sage on a hand-held drum and the barely audible strumming of Asha on her unplugged electric guitar. The two of them were sitting on a picnic table in the sun. Not that I had looked.

Dad threw his keys on the table and started unlacing his boots.

"How goes the ribboning?"

I held up an example of one perfect bow. "Brilliant," I said, with maybe a little too much sarcasm in my voice.

Dad sat down on a chair across from me. "I saw Sage and her friend in the park playing music."

I could feel my cheeks turning pink. "Yeah?"

"You know Jer," Dad said. "We sure appreciate you helping out with all this stuff. But you don't have to."

"I want to," I said, which was kind of true, kind of not.

"I've noticed you haven't talked about Sage this week," he said. "Last summer you always had a story to tell about her. What are you two up to this summer?"

I stacked a brown bar on a teal one. I tied it with ribbon. The lump rising in my throat was embarrassing. "You know. Not much."

"Because she found someone else?" he said. "That other girl?"

"Asha." I have to admit that I was kind of surprised. Dad didn't usually make observations like this about the people around him. I tied a perfect bow. "I don't really want to talk about it."

Dad nodded. "Well, if you ever do, you can always talk to Michael."

I looked up at him. His eyes were twinkling. We laughed because we both knew Dad wasn't much for sappy talk.

"Perfect," I said. "I'll do that."

CHAPTER

The morning of the Pride festival, Michael slid his plastic tote of rainbow things out from under the bed. There was even more crammed into it than last year. Several new hats, a rainbow collar that looked like a dog collar with metal spikes on it, and of course the standard bandanas, lanyards, boas, and t-shirts.

"What should I wear?" Michael asked, stirring the tote like a cauldron.

Dad picked up the leather collar. "This looks exciting," he said. "I think I might have an old leash from Cookie."

Michael snatched the collar from Dad. "Thanks, but no thanks. Either of you need anything to spruce yourselves up? Add a little glam?"

Dad and I were both just wearing boring old normal clothes, but also the baseball caps Michael bought us last year. Dad's had the bisexual flag on it. Mine had the word ALLY stitched in white.

Michael pulled out a bracelet of braided rainbow leather and asked Dad to help him clip it on. Then he pulled out a sparkly rainbow-striped fanny pack.

"Just when you thought fanny packs couldn't get any gayer," Dad grinned. "You never disappoint."

"Why thank you," Michael said.

And then we were off. I carried a bag with a large water bottle in it. I had learned from last year it was impossible to try to carry all the stuff the booths and vendors try to give you.

The day was overcast and there was a chance of rain. The clouds kept it from getting too hot, but it was stuffy in the mass of people in all the humidity. Michael immediately stopped for his giant cherry lemonade and almost as fast, we had to follow him to the port-a-johns. Some things never changed.

We joined the crowd of people walking past the rows of vendors. I got a notepad from Out Front Minnesota, a blue enamel pin with a yellow equal sign from the Human Rights Campaign, and a pack of Skittles from The Trans Youth Support Network. Right after spinning the prize wheel and winning a set of colored pencils from Dick's Art Supplies, someone called my name.

I turned around. Sage. She stood at the Hmong Pride table. Her bushy hair was tied up over her head like a fountain, or maybe a firework. Her mom, Lisa, stood with her. I didn't see her other mom, Reina, anywhere around.

"Happy Pride!" Sage called to me. Dad and Michael had already moved on ahead. I could see them talking to the people at the Open Arms table, their church. I passed through the stream of people to Sage's table. She came around to the front of the booth.

We stood for a minute. I could tell she had been about to give me a hug, but when it didn't happen, we were both frozen for a minute, unsure of what to do next. We just stared at each other. Sage wore a neon skirt with a zillion tiny pleats. It looked like the one she wore to Hmong New Year in the photo she showed me last year. But in the photo she had on necklaces and a hat and all sorts of other things, not just a t-shirt and flip flops.

"Where are your dads?" She asked.

Michael wasn't my dad yet. Not officially. I waved my hands towards them. "Off somewhere." We stared for another minute, then I turned to Lisa. "Happy Pride," I said.

"We haven't seen you around," Lisa said. "We've got a box of popsicles with your name on it. Swing by sometime."

"Yeah," I said. "Okay."

We stood for another minute. I turned to go.

"Wait," Sage said to me. Then she turned to Lisa. "Can I go with Jeremiah? For a while? I'll come back."

"Have fun," Lisa said, waving us away.

Sage walked next to me, so close our arms touched. You kind of had to walk that close in a crowd like this so you didn't get separated. Each time our arms touched, I felt a whoosh of gratitude. We were here. Together. But the image of Asha and Sage walking with their arms around each other's shoulders kept interrupting.

"Is Asha coming?" I asked. I couldn't help but feel jealous as I said her name.

"She said her dad doesn't like pride stuff and she doesn't like crowds." We walked past several booths for car insurance and home renovations that were giving out magnets. They felt out of place.

"Where have you been?" Sage asked. "I kind of thought maybe you were absorbed by a mutant blob or abducted by woodland sprites." She laughed.

"Pretty much," I said. I didn't like that she could laugh about it.

"I've missed you," she said.

I looked sideways at her. "Yeah? You should text me the next time you're doing something."

"Yeah," she said absently. "Ooh, look! I'll buy us some mini-donuts."

She grabbed my hand and pulled me towards the food booths. As we stood in line, I looked up at the grey sky. The air was getting thicker, tiny beads of moisture forming on us where we stood.

I pulled out my water bottle. After taking a long swig, I started to put it back in my bag.

"Care to share?" Sage asked.

I handed the bottle to her. She held it away from her mouth so it wouldn't touch her lips and poured it into her mouth.

"It looks like a storm's coming," I said.

Sage handed me the water bottle and looked up at the solid sky over our heads. "I have complete confidence that it will hold off. I can tell this cloud respects us. Maybe it just wants to give us a rainbow."

Sage stepped forward and paid for a bag of mini-donuts.

"What would you name it?" I asked.

"Name what?" She asked. "The mini-donuts?"

"No," I said. "The cloud."

Sage handed me a donut and smiled. "I can't think of a name big enough for this one."

She laughed and I laughed, which was maybe enough sunshine for now.

CHAPTER

"Oh my god, where were you?" Michael said. He ran up and grabbed my upper arms. I shrugged him off.

"I've just been hanging out with Sage," I said. She waved and popped the last mini-donut into her mouth.

Dad and Michael both said how good it was to see her, then turned back to me.

"We were worried about you, trooper," Dad said.

"Sorry," I said.

"Just tell us where you're going next time," Michael commanded.

"I've gotta get back to Mom and Hmong Pride," Sage said, probably to avoid the confrontation. "See you, Jeremiah."

We all waved.

"I'm old enough to be on my own," I said, refocusing on Dad and Michael. I was thirteen now, but they were still treating me like a kid.

"My stress levels are raging," Michael said, putting his hand to his forehead. "You could've been anywhere."

"Geez," I said. "I didn't even leave the park."

Michael took a deep breath. Then another one. "Allen?"

"Uh," Dad said. "Yeah. I'll take care of this." He sent Michael off to refill his cherry lemonade

Dad put his arm around my shoulder. We moved together through the crowd. "Wish it would rain," Dad said, guiding us out of the crowd to sit under a tree. It was an interesting thing to do considering there was no sunlight and therefore not really any shade. We both watched the people milling around the festival. "You're right, Jer. You're not a kid. It's hard for me to keep up with you. Every summer you're a full year older, but I don't get to watch you grow all year like your mom does."

"I know." I said. He looked sad about it. I hadn't expected that, somehow.

"Wow," he said. "I still can't believe you're thirteen. Thirteen. A teenager. And growing a mustache. I need to teach you to shave."

He *had* noticed. I liked the shadow over my top lip. I'd waited long enough for one to appear. I didn't want to lose it just yet.

"Is this shaping up to be a good summer for you?" Dad asked.

"Yeah," I said.

"Really, though, Jer," Dad said looking at me. "We've got all these teal canning jars and homemade soaps and seating charts. You need something outside of the mess. I'm pretty sure I'd go crazy if I didn't have work to get me away from all the doilies at least once a day."

"Yeah," I said, noncommittally.

"At least you've got Sage," Dad said, laying back on the grass. "Just like last summer."

"Yeah," I said.

Michael found us sitting under the tree. "Introverts at festivals," he laughed. "I don't know whether to think it tragic or adorable."

Michael pulled Dad to his feet. "I can hang with Jeremiah for a while," Michael said. "Go get yourself something."

I stood up. "We don't have to do everything together," I said. "I don't need anyone to babysit me."

"That's not what I meant," Michael said. "I just think that you should—"

"Let him," Dad said to Michael. "He's not a kid anymore. He's a young man."

Michael sighed, then turned to me. "Fine. But

you'll text us if you leave the park."

"Sure," I said.

"Can't hold on to them forever," Dad said as he and Michael walked hand in hand back into the crowd.

I leaned against the tree watching the people. Eventually, I decided to go back in, get some more stuff from the booths. I was halfway around the circle when I saw Reina, Sage's other mom, standing at a table for an organization called Bridge.

She wore a long sundress. Her straight red hair hung over her shoulders. A purple crystal pendant hung from a chain around her neck.

I went over to say hi.

I was surprised to see Robi standing behind the table next to Reina. They both greeted me, then turned to each other, laughing to compare how they both knew me.

"What's Bridge?" I asked.

Both of them started talking at once. Bridge was a place that helped refugees settle in

Minneapolis. They offered free English classes, job training, social services, and connected sponsors with new families to show them around the city. It met in the basement of Open Arms, Dad's and Michael's church.

"You're a teacher?" I asked Robi.

They shrugged. "I volunteer once a week in their community garden."

The two of them kept talking. Robi said that many people were fleeing countries where being on the LGBTQ spectrum can result in imprisonment or even death.

"Not that all of the refugees are queer, obviously," Reina chimed in. "We typically don't know one way or the other. It's not really our business to ask, but I always think of that when I'm working with new arrivals." Reina was intense as she spoke about this. Her eyes lit up the same way Sage's did.

"We're always looking for volunteers for the classroom," Robi said. "Summer session starts next Wednesday."

Maybe it was because of Robi and Reina standing there so inspired. Maybe it was because I wanted to get away from the mess of the wedding. Maybe it was because I was tired of riding around the neighborhood by myself.

When Reina held out the sign-up list for volunteers, I grabbed a pen and added my name.

CHAPTER

"What will you do at this volunteer thing?" Mom's voice echoed out of the speaker phone. My cell phone sat on the rocks next to me as I pulled weeds from around the daylilies and yellow *potentilla fruticosa* bushes in front of the apartment building.

"I don't know." It seemed like something I

probably should have clarified, but I figured any place at Bridge that I could be useful would be fine with me. And I'd find out in two days.

"You said it will be with Sage's mom?" Mom asked. "So you'll get more time with Sage."

Shifting the subject away from Sage, I picked something Mom couldn't resist: Michael's eating habits. "Michael is into this tea drink called kombucha. He makes it at home. There's a freaky mushroom thing in it."

"Sounds about right," Mom said. "You let me know if you need me to send you some old fashioned, wholesome, powdered lemonade."

I laughed. Truth be told, I actually really liked kombucha. It was sharp and alive on your tongue. Still, I wasn't about to admit that to Michael or to Mom. And that weird thing, he called a SCOBY, was a little freaky. It was like a pale, rubbery pancake that floated at the top of the jar. A symbiotic culture of bacterial yeast: SCOBY.

"I RSVP'd yes," Mom said.

I was still thinking about the SCOBY, so it took me a second to figure out what she'd just said. "To what?"

"The wedding, you ding-dong," Mom said. "I'll be coming in August."

"You're coming to Dad's wedding?" I said. "Won't that be weird for you?" I also wondered if it would be weird for Dad and Michael. And me. Yep, I was pretty sure it would be weird for me. Mom and Dad got along fine. As far as I could tell, the fact that they had divorced was the best thing for both of them.

Mom just laughed though. "Weird? Of course it is. Weird is the very definition of family. We divorced, but we don't hate each other. And we've got you. You keep us together, even though we're apart."

"No pressure or anything," I said.

"I even marked that I'll be bringing a plus one."

Well, this was news to me. "Who?"

"Zeb said he'd love to accompany me. He's

got family in Minneapolis he was planning on seeing later this summer anyway. We'll stay at his parents' cottage. We've been going to yoga together. And he offered to help me repaint the kitchen."

Mom had been going on the occasional date with my old second-grade teacher, Zebulon Wirtz, for the past several months. Apparently things were getting more serious now that school was out for the summer.

Mr. Wirtz was an awesome teacher. He was still one of my favorites. We basically spent half the year outside and all of our projects involved plants, rocks, and soil. As far as Mom's boyfriends went, he was good, but he also happened to have a three-year-old named Lila who looked like she'd just escaped a cotton candy explosion.

"What about Lila?" I asked.

"She'll spend the day with her grandparents. Speaking of grandparents and weird family, seeing Al's family is going to be a real bucket of daisies. But family is family. And some family you get to pick. Others, not so much."

"Grandma and Grandpa aren't coming to the wedding," I informed her. "And Aunt Paula and her family might not."

Mom sighed. "That shouldn't surprise anyone. But still, for God's sake! Religion. I don't get it."

"Not all religion," I said. "Dad and Michael take me to church." Open Arms had no problem with people on the LGBTQ spectrum. I was even starting to think their church was okay. Pastor Veronica always had funny stories in her homily, and there was an epic cookie table in the foyer afterwards.

"You're right," Mom said. "We can't homogenize." I heard her sigh, then add, "At least I'll be there. Al deserves to have real family attend."

CHAPTER

I sat on the stoop. My phone's notifications bar was as empty as the park in front of me.

The daylilies were budding.

"Whatever happened to all the pink ones?" Sage asked.

I looked up in surprise. "Hi," I said.

Sage knelt sat down on the stoop next to me.

As easily as if she'd been doing it all summer. As easily as if we'd never stopped since last summer. She looked at the strip of garden again. "I've been waiting for them to come back, but so far, they look all dried up."

"The petunias?" I said. Sage had chosen the little magenta flower as her contribution to the garden last year. "They were just annuals."

"Meaning?"

"They only live one year," I said. "Or one growing season actually. And then they die."

"Seriously?" Sage said, her eyes huge. "That's the worst. Why do people plant them if they're just going to wither up a few weeks later?"

I considered this. It was one of the reasons that I typically dealt in perennials, like the daylilies, that came back year after year. "Annuals usually bloom for a longer span of time. Like maybe spring, summer and fall, while most perennials just pick one season."

"So maybe they're more beautiful, but for not as long?" Sage said.

"Maybe," I said. "Definitely more loud and magenta, in the case of your petunias."

"Embrace the ephemeral," Sage said. "That's what one of my moms always says. Embrace the ephemeral."

Ephemeral being temporary.

I didn't want to embrace the ephemeral, though. That was what I'd done last summer with Mr. Keeler. I looked at Sage. I wanted things to be perennial.

"So no more petunias," Sage said with a sigh.

"The daylilies are doing well, though," I said. "They've got buds coming up and everything."

"Really?" Sage said, her shoulders straightening. "Let me see." She knelt in front of the grassy leaves of the daylilies. "Oh my gosh. Tiny baby flowers."

"Buds," I said.

"Yeah, those," she said. "Oh, they'll be so beautiful. I wish... I wish Mr. Keeler was here to see them."

"Me too." He was gone, but at that moment,

I still had Sage. I felt this way whenever we hung out, just the two of us, like nothing had changed. Like we were perennials.

"I talked to your Mom at Pride," I said.

"Which one?" Sage asked.

"Reina," I said. "I'm going to volunteer at Bridge with her."

"You'll have so much fun!" she said.

"Wanna volunteer with me?" I asked.

"I volunteer with her every day after school in the English class. I'm taking the summer off. But maybe I'll drop in sometime."

"Oh," I said. "Okay." This was a bummer. I mean, I'd decided to volunteer because I didn't just want to sit around all summer by myself. But still, it would've been nice.

I was just thinking that maybe I should run upstairs for the invitation when Sage looked past me, and her eyes lit up. "Asha!"

And just like that Sage ran to the girl in the glittering hijab. Asha did a cartwheel that ended in a somersault, sprang up, and somehow landed perfectly just inches from a full collision with Sage.

"I'm getting the hang of those cartwheel combos," Asha said casually, readjusting her hijab.

I couldn't believe how much she could do in a skirt. With the skinny jeans underneath, she was working around a lot of fabric.

"Guess what we got at Karmel today?" Asha said.

"You got it!" Sage yelped.

"Yep."

"Is it the most beautiful thing you've ever seen?" Sage said.

"Basically," said Asha.

And just like that I started to feel invisible again. "What did you get?" I asked a little loudly, maybe just to prove I still existed. "What's Karmel?"

"My burkini!" Asha said. "At Karmel, the Somali mall."

"What the heck is a burkini?" I asked.

"Her swimsuit," Sage explained. "It has more coverage. Modesty standards, you know?"

"Sure," I said.

"It's silvery green with sparkly patterns all down the sides," Asha said.

"You'll look like a mermaid," Sage said.

"You better believe I will," Asha said.

Sage started explaining the situation. "We've been waiting for her mom to finally buy her one so we can take swimming classes at the YWCA."

"Mom thinks shopping is annoying," Asha said. "But I dragged her there."

"With your mermaid power!" Sage said.

"Right," I said. "Mermaid power."

Sage turned towards me graciously. "You should totally join us. It took our combined powers and charm to get her parents to agree to a mixed class, but maybe it was fate."

"I already know how to swim," I said.

Sage frowned. "That's too bad."

"You want me to model it for you?" Asha asked Sage.

"Obviously!" Sage said. "See you around, Jeremiah!"

"Peace out," said Asha.

"Bye," I said back. Just like that I was alone again.

CHAPTER

With Sage gone and Michael in the middle of hand calligraphing the names for each place setting, I decided to go for a ride.

The garden center.

I would go to the garden center where Robi worked. Robi knew all about gardens. They would know what to do in place of the dead petunias.

I went inside the apartment building to the basement. My bike was sandwiched between Dad's tall bike and Michael's Uni-cycle.

Halfway through unlocking my bike, I stopped. My bike didn't have any way to transport stuff. No rack or basket. Dad's bike, on the other hand, had pannier baskets, one over each side of the rear wheel. He used it to pick up groceries sometimes. I looked up at the large ten-speed. I had outgrown my bike, yes, but I wasn't sure whether or not I was quite tall enough to handle Dad's bike. Only one way to find out.

Because Dad always used the same four digits, I had no trouble unlocking his bike. It was a lot lighter than I expected, not much heavier than mine, actually.

I wheeled it outside to the back alley and stood next to the curb while I buckled my helmet. I lowered the seat as much as it would go. With the help of the curb, I could swing my leg over the frame and just barely touch my toes to the ground if I really pointed my feet.

I was pretty sure Dad wouldn't care if I rode his bike around. He wasn't typically possessive about stuff like that. But if I crashed it, well, that was another story. Still, I figured as long as I didn't have to stop too much, I could make it to the garden center down Lyndale.

I started down the alley, watching for potholes. Dad said they were especially bad in Minnesota because of all the freezing and thawing between October and April.

I took the sidewalks up the hill on Franklin. Dad's bike was tall, but I could handle it. I stood into the pedals. It felt nice to be on a bike with enough room. I could really get my weight into each pedal unlike my own bike where my knees pumped up as high as my waist.

With the wind in my ears, I left all thoughts of Sage, Asha, and the wedding behind. The sun was warm. The air smelled like fresh grass and car exhaust mixed with all the garlic, onions, and oil from passing restaurants. It was an abundant smell.

When I made it to the garden center, I was sweating and thirsty, but in a good way. My skin prickled with sun and wind. I pulled over to a bike rack, jumped off the bike, and carefully locked it in place.

I walked into the garden center and breathed in the rich, heavy smell of wet earth and green plants. It was maybe my favorite smell in the universe. Maybe tied with the smell of libraries.

Robi had a hose in their hand, watering a rack of red geraniums. It was always interesting to see what Robi was wearing. Today, they wore a corduroy skirt and a black AC/DC t-shirt.

Robi smiled when they saw me. "Jeremiah," they said. "I was wondering when you'd pop on back here. How are the daylilies?"

"Budding," I said, thankful that they'd remembered. "But maybe not filling in as fast as I expected."

"What are you thinking, sir? Some mulch to keep the weeds down? Some fertilizer to help them fill out? Or maybe a few annuals to bloom in the blank spaces?"

"We did annuals last year," I said.

"Pink petunias, if I'm not mistaken," Robi said.

"Yeah." I was impressed. Did they remember this much about all the flowers that they sold? "But of course, the petunias are dead now."

"The tragedy of being an annual," Robi smiled.

"I've been meaning to pull out their dried-up stems and leaves. I don't like that they only last a year."

Robi turned off the hose. "Rather than pulling them out, you can just turn them under. They'll decompose into compost and feed the garden. Annuals only last a year, but you can enjoy them while they're there. And then bury what they leave behind to let them feed what's next."

"Embrace the ephemeral," I said. It was a little sarcastic, but Robi didn't seem to notice.

They smiled. "Exactly."

"Maybe a little fertilizer, and a few more annuals, then," I said.

I spent just about the rest of my allowance on a tub of organic plant food and half a flat of alyssum. I liked the alyssum. It was short and the flowers were white and fragrant. It was a lot mellower than the magenta petunias. I wondered whether Sage would think this new flower was too boring.

But Sage wasn't here.

Robi helped me nestle the plants into the bike baskets. "Best of luck on your agricultural adventure!" they said.

I climbed back up onto my bike. The ride home took a lot more concentration with the tottering weight of the flowers in my panniers. As I pedaled slowly but surely, I thought about annuals. Mr. Keeler had just been an annual. Last summer, I had hoped that Michael would be an annual, too. That he would leave. But by the end of the summer, that feeling changed. Now that he and Dad were getting married, he was going to be around year after year.

And what about Sage? Annual or perennial? I parked the bike in front of our building and started unloading the alyssum. My thoughts on annuals and perennials were interrupted.

"Hey." A boy rolled up next to me on his bike.

He'd surprised me. Maybe that's why I didn't say anything back. He looked familiar, but I couldn't say from what. He was taller than I was, had dark brown skin, short hair, a round belly. He watched me extract another flat of alyssum from the basket.

"That's a lot of flowers you've got," he said. "What are they for?"

"My flower garden." I waved my hand towards the daylilies and *potentilla fruticosa*. I could feel my face turn a little pink. I wasn't embarrassed by the fact that I worked on a flower garden, but sometimes other kids my age, especially boys, thought this kind of thing was stupid. I probably should've just said, *garden*, instead of *flower garden*.

"You have a flower garden?" he said.

"Yeah, I do," I said, maybe just a little too loudly.

"Oh," he said, raising his eyebrows. "Cool." I couldn't tell whether he was mocking me or not. His smile didn't seem like a mocking smile, but it could be hard to be sure about something like that. His eyes were so bright and smiley that I was pretty sure I'd interpreted him wrong. I wanted to say something to let him know that I didn't mean to react so defensively. That I was just surprised.

We just stood and stared at each other for what felt like a long time, but was probably only a few minutes or even moments. What was I supposed to say next? I was never good at the whole chatting with random people thing.

"I'm Asad," he said.

"Hi." My brain tried to calculate what to say back. "Nice to meet you."

Another silence.

"Okay," he said. "Have fun."

"Yeah," I said.

He rode off. As he did, I noticed that his bike was pink. I recognized it. It was the bike that Asha rode. She'd mentioned that she had to share it with her brother. That's why I recognized him. I had seen him on the morning we went to the Mall of America.

All of a sudden, I felt like I'd missed an opportunity. An opportunity for what I wasn't sure. Maybe to try for another friend. I wondered why I hadn't been friendlier. I replayed the conversation in my head and realized I hadn't even told him my name back.

I wanted to call out to him, but he was already turning the corner.

CHAPTER 12

My first morning volunteering at Bridge was cloudy, but bright. Like the day didn't quite know whether it was going to turn to rain or break into sunshine.

"Bring an umbrella with you," Michael said. "Just in case." He was sitting at the kitchen table pulling faded artwork out of a pile of frames he'd bought at a thrift store. The idea was to paint the frames in the wedding colors. The guests could hold them up and pose inside the frame to take selfies while they waited in line to eat.

"I don't need an umbrella," I said. "It's just a few blocks." I shut the door before he could argue, and ran down the stairs off towards the Bridge classrooms in the basement of Open Arms.

I opened the heavy door to the old brick church and went downstairs to the community room. A bunch of people were gathering in two of the classrooms. I didn't see Robi, so I went to the classroom with Reina inside. She greeted me and told me I could pick a seat at one of the tables that formed a horseshoe around her.

Pocket charts full of sight words, maps of the world, and the days of the week hung on the walls. Most of the items in the room were labeled. Like a big sticker that said "phone" on the telephone, "marker" on each of the dry-erase markers. "Chair." "Table." "Light switch." The back of the room was a wall of book shelves crammed with magazines, workbooks, alphabet puzzles, and containers of crayons. I wondered whether this room was also used for Sunday school sometimes.

The class was made of five students who were more diverse than I had expected. Asli's wrinkled brown face was framed by her hijab. Nur, who wore a round cap and a suit jacket. The two of them were Somali*. There was an Asian dude named Marner Saw in what looked like a sarong. He was Karen*, from Burma or Myanmar. Mustafa was from Iraq; his skin was lighter brown and he smelled like cloves and tobacco. And Ifaa, who had very dark brown skin, and a huge smile full of crooked teeth, was Oromo*. Even though summer was starting to heat up, he wore a long- sleeved button down and a suit jacket.

"Students," Reina said. "Good morning."

*Somalis are an ethnic people from Somalia; Karen are an ethnic people from Myanmar; Oromo are an ethnic group from Eastern Africa

"Good morning, Teacher," the students said back. All of those voices and accents and different timings gave the practiced response texture.

"This is Jeremiah," Reina said. "He is a volunteer."

I could feel my cheeks getting red. "Hi," I said. I wasn't sure whether I should say something more. I didn't know how much the students would understand.

Ifaa, who was sitting next to me, reached out and we shook hands.

I was thankful when class started so I could focus on something besides my burning face and uncertainty. The class was slow-paced. Not in a boring way, but maybe a gentle way. Reina gave time for silence after asking questions. We read things slowly. We wrote things just as slowly. After writing the date and talking about what we did the night before ("Eat. Watching TV. Go to sleep," said Nur), we talked about jobs.

Reina projected images onto the screen and

the students talked about what the job was. A doctor, a bus driver, a postal worker, a farmer.

"I am a teacher," Reina said.

"I am a teacher," several of the students repeated.

"Me," Reina pointed to herself. "I am a teacher."

"Ah, yes," Ifaa said. "You are a teacher."

"What is your job?" Reina asked.

Several people repeated the question, but Asli seemed to understand. "My job," she said. "My job in Ethiopia. I am cooking food. Restaurant."

"Okay," Reina said, writing Chef and Cook on the board and reading the words to the class.

"Chef," everyone repeated. "Cook."

"Thank you. Who else? What is your job?"

"Nurse," said Ifaa. "At the hospital."

"Nurse," Reina wrote on the board.

Marner Saw, the guy in the sarong, said, "Elephants. Standing. Dancing. Elephant teacher."

Holy crap.

"Elephant trainer," Reina wrote.

When class ended, I helped by erasing the board and pushing in the chairs.

"How was your first day?" Reina asked as she gathered up her laptop and the extra worksheets and put them into her canvas tote. "You'll do more hands-on stuff in the future, but I wanted you to get a feel for how class works."

"It wasn't what I expected," I said. "They weren't what I expected."

"What did you expect?" Reina asked.

"I don't know." I tried to put my finger on it. "When I thought about refugees, I guess maybe I imagined people escaping through a jungle or something. Not a nurse, or chef. And definitely not an elephant trainer."

Reina smiled. "Some of these people have escaped through jungles and many have experienced trauma. But those are things that have happened to them, not who they are inside. I wish more people understood that."

Reina took me to the other classroom.

A man walked over. I later found out that he was Somali, too. Reina introduced him as Taban.

"Hi," I said, extending my hand. "I'm Jeremiah."

"Are you a volunteer?" he asked.

I nodded.

"The beginning class is a lot of fun," he said. "They make so much progress so quickly."

"Some of the time," laughed Reina.

"Yes," Taban agreed. "I hope you enjoy it."

I was impressed with how clear his English was. Apparently, there was a big difference between Reina's class and whatever level he was in. "Your English is very good," I told him.

He laughed. So did Reina. "Thank you," Taban said. "I hope you're right. I'm one of the teachers here."

I could feel my face getting hot. Wow. Nice.

"Oh," was all I could think to say. But neither of them had made a big deal about it. They transitioned the conversation to who was going to drive the Bridge van around to pick up the students the next day.

My face cooled back down by the time that they settled the situation and I waved goodbye, following Reina up the stairs and out the door.

Reina walked back to the apartment with me. The sun had broken through the morning clouds. The sky was bright blue. It was warm, but there was a breeze. The world felt alive.

When we got back to the apartment, Reina said, "I'll see you tomorrow?"

"You bet," I said.

Just as we were about to part ways, Michael waved to us from the park, beckoning us towards him. Reina and I both went over. He had what I recognized as the seating chart for the wedding. He treated it like a puzzle. Like a game of Tetris where there was a spot for everyone if he just figured out how to twist and arrange them all.

Michael and Reina exchanged hellos.

"How is this guy at volunteering?" Michael

asked with a smile.

Reina laughed. "I think we'll take him. What are you working on?"

Michael held up the paper. "Seating chart for the wedding."

"Fun," Reina said.

"Super fun," Michael said. "So much fun. The most fun ever. Especially because we're still waiting for everyone to RSVP."

He managed to say this lightly, but there was a kind of expectancy in his voice. He was looking meaningfully at Reina. He apparently thought that I'd given them the invitation.

My ears got hot as I looked between them, thinking of the invitation buried in my sock drawer, but I didn't say anything.

CHAPTER

Planting the alyssum around the daylilies gave me something to do, but, like watering the garden, it only lasted so long. Not long enough. I helped Michael finish framing the little name place markers. I learned how to make a new special kind of bow so I could tie chocolate-brown ribbon around the teal jars for the centerpieces.

Volunteering at Bridge gave me something to look forward to. I liked the routine of Reina's classroom. Every day we started with a date worksheet. *Today is... Yesterday was... Tomorrow will be...* Then we did a letter of the day, writing the lowercase and uppercase. Reina asked the class for three words starting with that letter, and we'd spell them on the board.

It took me a while to get used to the amount of wait time. "Wait time" was a new term I learned from Reina, although it means pretty much what you'd expect. Having good wait time meant waiting patiently and silently while students thought of the answer instead of answering your own question to appease the uncomfortable silence. If we waited long enough, somebody always had an answer, even if it might not have been the one we'd expected.

One of my primary jobs was to be what Reina called, "The example student." When she was demonstrating what to do in a new activity, she and I would role play what was happening next. I was the first to answer, then ask the next person a question around the circle: "What color is your shirt?" "How are you today?" "What do you eat?" She had me demonstrate how to do the flyswatter game where you had to smack the correct word on the board after Reina said it. I would describe one thing I saw on the picture projected on the screen. She'd throw the ball to me first and I would say, "I want the ball," or, "I don't want the ball." Stuff like that.

Being around new people was always awkward for me, but I was starting to get used to the group. It was a lot easier to start to feel comfortable since we were in a structured environment. I was starting to enjoy each of the students.

Asli was always super serious and focused. Nur looked grumpy but his scowl could turn to a smile in a nanosecond if he answered something correctly. Mustafa often came into the classroom singing. All through class he would tap out soft rhythms onto the table, which clearly annoyed Nur. Marner Saw acted quiet and didn't often speak up, but I could see him mouthing the right answers to himself all through class, and he was lightning fast with his Karen-English dictionary. And Ifaa was a bit of a know-it-all. Every class needs one of those.

I had started volunteering at Bridge with some vague idea of how sad and insurmountable it must be for these people to have to learn a new language for the first time in a strange country. Then, on one of the first days I was in the class, I looked over at Asli's notebook. The page she had open was packed with writing. At first glance I thought she had bad handwriting. I couldn't recognize the letters. Then I looked closer.

She was writing in a different alphabet. A different language.

I pointed to her notebook. "Somali?"

She shook her head. "Arabic," she said.

I raised my eyebrows. "Three languages?" I

ticked them off on my fingers. "Somali. Arabic. English."

She smiled. "Yes."

Nur, who was watching us, held up four fingers. "Somali. Arabic. Italian. English."

Holy crap.

Marner Saw was watching us. "Four," he said. "Karen. Karenni. Thai. English."

Not about to be outdone, Ifaa held up five fingers, but I didn't get to learn which ones he knew because we had to move on to the next activity. Mustafa smiled at me and held up three fingers.

Dang. And I thought learning Spanish was hard.

These people were my favorite part of volunteering, but my second favorite part was the community garden.

Tuesdays were garden days. On my first Tuesday before class started, Reina led me down the side of Open Arms to the garden space nestled behind the church. The garden space was bigger than I would have expected back there.

"Many of our students grew their own food at one point or another," Reina said. "But most now live in apartments where it is difficult for them to continue that practice."

"Yeah," I said. "I get that."

A person with a handful of weeds stood amidst the garden beds. "Robi!" I said.

Robi laughed. "Howdy."

"Well, I'll leave you two to it," Reina said. "I've got to go see if the copier is finally working."

Robi showed me around the garden. There were four rectangular raised beds. I recognized most of the plants. Tomatoes, squash, onions. But there were some that Robi had to tell me. Okra, eggplant.

Everything was kind of mixed, with multiple types of plants in the same beds. It seemed cluttered. Chaotic.

"Why are the plants so crowded and mixed up?" I asked. If I were to plant a vegetable garden, I thought it would probably be one of those with long rows of a single type. This is the tomato row. The line of peas. Beans. Etc.

"Companion planting," Robi said.

"What?" I asked.

Robi brushed the dirt off their hands. "Companion planting is where you put plants together that nourish and support each other. Some return nutrients to the soil that the other one needs. Some repel pests that would harm their neighbors. Over here, we've got basil growing with the tomatoes to increase yield and keep the flies off. Beans with the cabbages to restore nitrogen. Onions with carrots to keep away the aphids. You get the idea."

"Cool," I said. It was. I had never heard of such magic.

"It helps the plants thrive instead of just survive," Robi said. "Plants can be like people: not much on their own, but everything together."

I liked that idea.

After a shorter class, Reina led the students

out to the garden. Marner Saw, seeing that the tomatoes and peas were starting to vine over the soil, went to a pile of sticks and selected a few sturdy branches. He shoved them into the soil and several students bent forward to twist the plants upward off the dirt, using the sticks like trellises to give them something to climb on. I'd only ever seen people keep tomatoes up with tomato cages.

Mustafa pointed at the trellis sticks, laughed, and said, "Recycling."

"Yeah," I said. "Recycling."

I helped a few students turn the compost pile with pitchforks. "Last year: garden," Asli said. "Next year: soil."

I thought again about what Robi had told me about not tossing out the old annuals, but turning them under to enrich the soil. They never really leave. The old keeps enriching what is here and now.

CHAPTER

One night at the beginning of July, Dad and I rode our bikes down the Greenway towards Lake Bde Maka Ska in Uptown. The traffic was slow enough on the bicycle highway for us to ride next to each other. It was hard to keep up on last year's bike.

"You've been spending a lot of time at that

class, Michael tells me," he said.

"Yeah," I said. "I like it."

He turned his gaze from the road in front of him. "I'm proud of you, Jer."

"Thanks," I said. I stood up on my pedals to keep up.

Dad slowed down. "We need to get you a new bike, huh?"

"I'm okay," I said.

"We'll do it just as soon as I get a chance. Maybe this weekend."

"Okay," I said.

"But not tomorrow. Tomorrow is the Fourth of July. Ready for fishing?"

Dad and I had been fishing on the Fourth of July since before I was old enough to hold my first Snoopy fishing pole.

While Dad and I had the tradition of fishing on Independence Day, Michael had his own tradition: the "Freedom from Pants" ride. A group of people met in the park outside our apartment for a bike ride through Minneapolis without pants, wearing all sorts of crazy boxers, tutus, and whatnot. Why? I had no idea. I was thankful Dad and I had a tradition that took us as far away from that as possible. I could celebrate freedom with pants on, thank you very much.

I remembered what Reina had told the class that morning about the holiday. "Tomorrow is the Fourth of July," Reina said at the beginning of class when we were writing the date. "The Fourth of July. The birthday of the United States. On the Fourth of July, people use fireworks." She held up a small firecracker, then a larger firework. She projected images of fireworks onto the screen, then switched to a YouTube video of fireworks exploding. "There will be many fireworks."

She reviewed the fireworks again at the end of the day before the students left.

"Why did you talk so much about the fireworks?" I asked.

"Many of our students have lived through

military conflict. Imagine that you've lived through something like that and all of a sudden the world outside your home sounds like you're being bombed. The Fourth of July can be very triggering to some students."

Dad and I came to a hill and let our bikes coast down.

"Maybe we'll catch a fish this year," I said to Dad.

Dad laughed. "With our track record, I'd be surprised."

When Dad and I rode up to the building later, Sage and Asha saw us and ran over to say hi.

"I'll leave y'all to talk," Dad said, giving me a smile and a wink. He lifted his bike up the steps and disappeared into the building.

"So," I said. I didn't really know what to say. "Um."

But of course, Sage didn't leave a silence for that long. She burst out an invitation to join her family at J4, a huge Hmong celebration in Saint

Paul on the Fourth of July. "And guess who else is gonna be there?" she asked.

I was pretty sure I already knew the answer to that one. "Asha?"

Asha laughed. "Guilty."

"Sorry," I said and told them about my tradition fishing with Dad.

"Tragic," Sage said. "We'll be back for fireworks, though."

I told her what Reina had said about the fireworks that morning. I wanted to hear what Sage thought, but mostly I wondered what Asha would say.

"Yep," Asha said. "My parents are refugees. My dad wears earplugs all night on the Fourth of July. But my mom buys all the fireworks she can. She's a pyromaniac. Like the really big ones. You need to come outside our building tomorrow and see."

"You just have to," Sage said, her face shining. "It will be so epic!"

"Maybe," I said.

"Come on," Sage begged. "You can't avoid us forever or we're gonna think you don't like us."

I made myself give a little laugh. "Maybe," I repeated.

Sage and Asha looked at each other, then back at me with overexaggerated pouts. "Pwetty pwease."

I made a gagging noise. "Fine," I said. "Only if you agree to never talk like that again."

The both of them laughed. "Deal." Off they walked arm in arm, giggling to each other.

I wasn't sure whether or not I was happy to go to their fireworks. I liked being asked, but I didn't know whether going would be worth anything.

But, I guess, there was only one way to find out.

CHAPTER

Dad and I woke up early, dug the fishing poles and tackle box from the back of the closet, and grabbed an empty cooler. I climbed up into the cab of the truck. We drove into the dawn, stopping at a gas station for Boss subs loaded with meat. I picked out one of those giant cans of Arizona iced tea. Dad grabbed a bottle of coconut water. Last year, we'd grabbed two Mountain Dews. I guess our tastes were changing. But we still got a box of powdered sugar donuts and coffees for breakfast.

We left the city behind.

Bayport was a small town on the banks of the Saint Croix river. We found a spot alongside the wide, slow river that sparkled in the early morning sun.

We sat on the pier for a long time, just watching the river. Casting. Watching our bobbers float with the current. The bitter coffee and sweet donuts made a perfect pair. Maybe like the phrase Robi had said about the companion planting. Not much on their own, but everything together. Companion foods. That could be a thing, right?

I laughed to myself.

Dad looked at me. "What's so funny?"

I shrugged. "Coffee and donuts."

He laughed, too. The water lulled us into silence. Not an awkward silence. A comfortable one. It lasted a long time before Dad broke it with a question.

"How's your summer going, Jer?" he asked.

I wasn't sure how to answer him. It was fine, I guess. It had become fine. I was going to say that it was a lonely summer, but somehow that wasn't entirely true any more. I had thought that the summer was going to be full of Sage, but that just wasn't how things were shaping up. Now I had Bridge.

"It's going fine," I finally settled on.

"Just fine?" Dad asked.

"It's been a little lonely," I admitted. I ate another donut, licking the powder from my fingers. "But fine. And fine is good. Things are just… different. Different this year."

"Well, that's to be expected," Dad said. "You're growing up, Jeremiah. Thirteen. Dang. Everything starts changing at thirteen. You know I had my first girlfriend at thirteen." He poked me. I blushed a little. "You're not a kid anymore."

I hadn't exactly felt like a kid last summer either. Or the summer before that. When exactly had I last felt like a kid?

"You know, my Dad never talked to me about things like growing up," Dad said. "Or how the body changes. How your feelings change. Or you start to get attractions. I don't really know how to do that." He scratched behind his ear. His cheeks turned a little bit darker. "I guess, do you have any questions?"

I knew where this was going. Mom had given me a book called *Just Us Guys* that had answered most of my questions about bodily changes and hormones and wet dreams and stuff. Reading about it was one thing, but talking to Dad felt a little weird.

I ate another donut, and cast my line far out into the river. My bobber flowed slowly south.

I actually did have a question, though. "When did you know about yourself?"

Dad twitched his line. "What do you mean?"

"You know. When did you figure out that you

were bisexual? How did you figure it out?"

Dad took a swig of coffee. "That's a tough one. Let's see." He ate the last donut. "Well, have you ever heard that hindsight is 20/20?"

"Yeah."

"It is kind of like that for me. I can look back and see signs that I was bi from a young age. But I didn't know it at the time. You have to understand, your grandparents kept a tight hold on us. We were raised the children of conservative religious people in a small, conservative religious town. I had no idea bisexuals even existed. From everything I'd been taught, there was only one kind of person in the world: straight people. I knew I had feelings towards both guys and gals. I figured everybody did. But there was only one thing to do with those feelings, wait them out until I married a woman."

"Which you did," I said.

Dad reeled in his line. "Which I did. But not until after I'd figured it out. It wasn't until

I got a job in Billings that I realized that gay people existed. It was the first time I'd ever met or realized that people had attraction to their same gender. Well, I knew I was like that. I was attracted to men, so I came out of the closet as gay."

"As gay?" I was surprised. He'd always been bisexual as far as I knew.

Dad laughed. "Funny, isn't it? Identity is a river. It can change and flow, but all the time you're still you."

"Wow," I said. "That's pretty profound."

He laughed again. "It is, isn't it? I read it in one of those inspirational books on Robi and Em's coffee table." He flicked his fishing pole and sent his lure soaring back over the water. We watched our lines. The sun was getting warmer. Not hot yet.

"So," I prompted him. "You came out as gay."

"And your grandparents just about had heart attacks," he said, laughing again. But from the way he laughed, I could tell he didn't think it was funny. "They insisted nobody was gay. Some people were just confused. Well, I knew they were wrong. I was just finally getting past my confusion. Although I still didn't get why, if I was gay, I had feelings for women, too. The other gay guys I knew didn't seem to get it. Honestly, it wasn't until I met your mother that I finally figured out what had been driving me crazy. I was just bi."

"So, she knew you the whole time as bisexual?"

He shook his head. "She knew me when I still introduced myself as gay. She was there when I started calling myself bi."

I reeled in my line and stretched the pole across my knees so I could focus on the story. "What did Grandpa and Grandma think about it?"

"Which ones? My parents or your mom's?"

I shrugged. "Both."

Dad shook his head. "My parents swore that my spirit was getting healed when I told them I was marrying your mother. They thought I was finally accepting that I was straight. Your mom's parents? Well, they swore that I was actually gay and would leave her one day. People have a hard time sometimes accepting that a person is actually bi, and not just denying that they're gay or straight."

"That sucks." It was the best thing I could think of to say. From what he'd said, I was pretty sure that it was just plain true.

Dad sighed. "Parents are sometimes the most difficult crowd to please, that's for sure. Would you agree?"

"Maybe." I said.

Dad's line gave a jolt. His pole bent as he quickly reeled in his line. The first catch of the day. I sprang up for the net. But then we saw his lure had just snagged some sort of green plant from the depths. He pulled it up out of the water. "Look, I caught something for Michael. A vegetarian-friendly fish."

Dad and I laughed as we unhooked the

tangled mass. "Do you think we'll have to scale it before we filet?" I said.

We dropped the green bundle back into the river. I grabbed Dad's lure and picked out the leaves.

"People still do it," Dad said.

"Do what?"

"Try to put me in the category of gay or straight. Even other queer people."

I thought about this. "Like mom calling bisexual, 'Diet Gay?'"

"Exactly like that."

"I know it's not," I said. "You're you, through and through."

Dad clapped me on the shoulder. "Thank you, Jer. And as you keep discovering who you are, know that I support the heck out of you."

"Thanks," I said. I knew he meant it.

Dad pulled me into a side hug. "You'll keep changing and I'll have to try to keep up with you."

"I don't like change," I said.

Dad laughed. "You never have. But you know what they say: the only constant is change."

By mid-afternoon we still hadn't caught anything long enough or fish enough to keep. Fishing was our tradition, but going home empty-handed was becoming just as much of a tradition. But for us, fishing wasn't really about getting fish. It was about more than that. It was about exactly what had happened on the dock today.

Terrell texted me. *Happy 4th.* My phone gave me the notification that it couldn't download his picture or gif or whatever he'd added. *Fishing?*

I texted him back. *Yep. Just caught a dolphin.*

lol tell me how it tastes

"Who's that?" Dad asked, nodding to my phone.

"Terrell," I said.

"You miss your friends back home?"

I swallowed. "Yeah." I wanted to say that I missed having a friend here. But I didn't.

When we got back to the city, we went to Brit's Pub for fish and chips with Michael.

"Ready for fireworks, you two?" Michael asked as we wolfed down the best fish and chips I'd had since last year at Brit's.

I thought about my promise to Sage and Asha. It seemed like a stupid choice at this point, but maybe it would be okay. It could be fun. Maybe.

"Instead of going down by the river this year," I said, "Could we go somewhere else?"

Dusk was closing in.

A bunch of people gathered in the parking lot outside of Asha's building, including Sage and her moms. I met Asha's mother and was finally formally introduced to her brother, Asad. I had been right. He was the guy who'd talked to me when I was unloading the flowers from the garden center.

"We've met," Asad said. "Kind of. You're the flower dude."

I smiled. "That's me."

"It was an awkward meeting," Asad said. His twinkling eyes met mine, and we both laughed, as if the memory was something funny instead of an embarrassing reminder that I could be kinda lousy at meeting new people.

"He's my twin brother," Asha said, pulling Asad into a side hug.

"I didn't know you were twins," I said.

"You never asked," Asha laughed.

"We're the twinsiest twins that ever twinned," Asad said.

We laughed. Asha introduced everyone to her mother, who said, "Hello. No English."

"That's what she always says," Asad said. "But she can speak a lot of English. She's getting her GED."

An alarm went off on one of their phones.

"We'll be right back," Asha said. "Sunset. Time to pray."

The three of them went into the building. Dad and Michael started chatting with Sage's moms.

Sage turned to me and started telling me a long story about all the things she and Asha had done and seen at J4. I gave noncommittal grunts. Enough to show I was listening, but I just didn't have anything to add or say back. I swatted a mosquito that landed on my arm.

"I wish you would've come," she said when her story was through. "But I'm glad you came tonight. I was afraid you wouldn't. You've been invisible lately. Where have you been?"

I felt awkward. "You and Asha..."

Sage looked at me like she was trying to figure out a puzzle. "Me and Asha what?"

I drew a line in the gravel at the edge of the parking lot with my shoe. "You just. You. You know." I looked up at her. She didn't look like she knew. "You're just always doing everything together." I blurted out the last sentence.

"Well yeah," Sage said. "Asha's my best friend."

There it was. She'd said it herself.

She looked hard at me. "I mean, you're my

best friend, too, right?"

"Sure," I said. Of course, she would be the kind of person to have more than one best friend. Sage probably had whole armies of best friends. "Okay," I said, then bit my lip. I forced out the words, "Text me next time you hang out?"

"Lovely," Sage said. She pulled me into a hug. I could feel my cheeks getting hot, but I hugged her back.

"What?" Asha said, coming back towards us. "You're hugging without me? Group hug."

"Oh my god," I said, as I got swallowed in their arms.

Asad was watching us. He smiled at me, and rolled his eyes at his sister.

Asha's mom yelled something in Somali.

Asha sighed. "She said to stop hugging boys. But sometimes I just can't help it." She laughed as the hug unraveled.

Asad introduced me to his father, who was even taller than Dad. He had a goatee that was starting to turn grey. He wore a sort of robe or really long shirt, a hat, and a pair of orange earplugs that made him talk super loud.

"All this fire," he said, nodding towards his wife. "It's dangerous."

"Yeah," I said when he turned to me. "It is."

"America," he said, shaking his head, but smiling. "Home of the brave."

I laughed. So did he.

"Hey," Asad called. "She's starting!"

Their mom had a lighter stick and hopped between the fireworks holding her hijab back from the flames. The wicks caught and fizzed. She ran to the edge of the parking lot with a laugh and a yell. Flame and sparks shot up and whistled through the twilight.

Asad stood next to me as we faced the firework display. Other people were adding to it now. Rockets and fountains and sparklers lighting up the night. It wasn't anything like the huge fireworks down by the river, but it was dazzling in its own way.

As each of the fireworks started spouting

fountains of sparks or shooting up into the air, their mom cheered and clapped. She thrust extra-long sparklers into all of our hands and lit them. I hadn't held a sparkler since I was a little kid.

"Sorry," Asad said. "She can be kinda embarrassing."

I looked over at Michael who was waving his sparkler in the air in a sort of dance, his hips swinging wide. I looked back at Asad.

"She's awesome," I said, and waved the sparkler over my head. "Trust me, you have nothing to be embarrassed about."

CHAPTER

I was on another pointless afternoon ride around the neighborhood. Sage still hadn't texted me. I knew I could text her, but I wanted her to contact me first. I still thought it would prove something. The sun beat down until I was sweaty all over and my bike felt harder and harder to pedal. Spotting the library up ahead, I decided to take a break.

I locked my bike. As I opened the door, a delicious wave of cold air and chattering voices blew over me. The Franklin Library always buzzed with noise. Not in a loud obnoxious way, just in a way that felt alive. After billowing my shirt to dry off my armpits and back, I sat down at an open computer and checked my email. Besides the occasional email with Sage over the past school year, I never got anything. But having an email account still felt like an important step towards being an adult.

Today I actually did get something. It was a forward from my Aunt Beth titled, INSPIRATIONAL STORY ABOUT STARFISH. I went ahead and deleted it. She had a tendency to pass along her spam.

I logged out and flipped through a few magazines. I read an article in *National Geographic* about the aftereffects of the Syrian refugee crisis. Now that I was aware of the idea of refugees, stuff about them caught my eye. I picked out a couple of DVDs. They had the new DC superhero movie. I scanned Dad's library card and checked out.

On the ride home, my bike was going slower than normal, and I was having to work a lot harder. I thought it was because the way home was mostly uphill.

I stood up on the pedals, then finally looked down. My back tire was flat.

"Dang it," I said. It wasn't that long of a walk home, but it was definitely long enough that pushing my bike the whole way was going to suck. I squished the tire. It gave easily to my grip. I must have run over something and punctured it on my way to the library and let the air leak out. No wonder it had felt harder and harder to pedal. And now it was empty. "All because I wasted time on checking my email," I muttered.

I took off my helmet and clipped it to the handlebars. I didn't need any extra layer to sweat into. I had just passed Chicago Ave when someone yelled behind me. On Franklin you learn to ignore the occasional shout. But when they yelled again, I realized they were shouting my name.

I turned around. A familiar face rode towards me on a bike. It took me a minute to connect the face to the person. It was Asad, Asha's brother, pedaling Asha's pale pink bike. Beads of sweat stood out on his forehead. It didn't surprise me. He was wearing a backpack over a purple, long-sleeved Minnesota Vikings shirt. He smiled that huge smile at me.

"Hey," he said.

"Hi," I said.

We just stared at each other for a minute.

Then he broke the silence. "Wanna ride back together? I was just at the market picking up bananas and rice."

I explained about my bike. He got off his and took a look.

"You have a patch kit?"

"No," I said. "Although I'm starting to think

that I should just keep an extra tire in my back pocket."

He laughed. "I got you covered."

We crossed the street to a park and found an unoccupied pool of shade under a linden tree.

Asad pulled a pouch of bike tools out of the front pocket of the backpack. He showed me how to remove the back wheel and lever the back tire off, leaving the floppy inner tube behind. He inflated it and held it close to his ear as he rotated it.

"Here," he said, holding it towards my own ear. "Hear it hissing?"

I held it close. "Yeah."

He slowly examined the tire itself until he found a shard of glass that had wedged its way through the tough rubber. He handed it over to me so I could wiggle out the glass while he moved back to the inner tube.

"Now for the patch kit." He opened a little box with wipes to clean the innertube before fusing on the patch. His hands worked fast and purposefully.

"You've done this once or twice," I said.

"A few hundred times," he said. "Asha is always running our bike over broken glass, old nails, the occasional short sword."

I laughed.

He patted his bike as if it were a horse. "You poor thing. But that's what happens when you have to share a bike with your twin. Do you have brothers or sisters?"

I shook my head. "None."

"Lucky," he laughed. "I'm saving for a new bike. My parents aren't pitching in since I'm the one that forgot to lock it. I'm not even halfway yet."

"That sucks," I said.

He showed me how to use the little pocket pump and reassemble the wheel. We tightened the bolt back onto the bike.

"You'll want to give it a pump with a real bike pump when you get back," he said. "But it will get you back."

"Thanks," I said. "Seriously."

"No problem," he said. "I'm kinda the superhero of flat tires."

We both laughed. It felt good to laugh without having to think about it.

My phone buzzed. It was Sage. *Parkour in the park. Lazy vaults.*

I had no idea what lazy vaults were, but I didn't need to just then. The fact that she'd texted made me feel, what was it? Relief? Warmth?

Asad looked from me to the phone. "Need to go?"

"Just a second," I told him. I texted her back, *Maybe next time.*

She sent me a thumbs up.

I tucked my phone into my pocket. I looked up and saw Asad smiling at me.

"Race you back," he said. "On your mark—" Then he kicked off.

"Hey," I yelled, riding after him.

Bike racing in the city is different from racing

in the suburbs or in the country. You have to stop at each light, so you really keep restarting every time you get a walk sign. As we kept passing each other, I could tell that his bike was too small for him, too. But he was pretty fast. I stood up on my pedals to keep up with him up the hill.

We were both soaked with sweat when we got back to our neighborhood. When we got to the park, Sage and Asha were running, planting their hands on a picnic table and swinging their legs out to the side in a way that swung over and across the top of the table.

Asad and I stopped, watching them while we caught our breath.

"I think I owe you an apology," Asad said, turning away from them to face me.

"What?" I said. "Why?"

His eyes twinkled. "Because I destroyed you in that race. I bet it hurt."

We both laughed. The sound of our laughter made Sage and Asha look in our direction. The two of them waved. We waved back.

"I hate parkour," Asad said.

"Thank God." I laughed.

"It's not funny," Asad said, but he was smiling. "But seriously. Asha already smashed my lamp, destroyed our coffee table, and kicked a foot-sized hole through her bedroom wall."

"Wanna try?" Sage yelled to us.

"Maybe next time," I yelled back.

"Maybe never!" Asad yelled.

I was worried that might hurt their feelings, but Asha called, "Boring butts!" And the two of them just laughed and went back to their lazy vaults.

Asad rolled his bike towards them. I sighed, then followed. As we watched, I had to admit they were actually getting pretty skilled. Asad clapped at a perfectly executed move by Asha. Then one by Sage.

The sight of them launching through the air and laughing together didn't hurt right now. Not next to Asad.

Asad and I watched them for a few more minutes. I was trying to figure out what was supposed to happen next. I tried to think of something funny to say, but I can't ever find something funny when I'm trying.

"Well," I finally said.

"Yeah," Asad said. He pointed his thumb over his shoulder to the backpack. "These bananas and rice aren't going to deliver themselves."

"Alright," I said, starting to roll towards my building. "I should..." But I didn't know what I should do. I just kept wheeling towards the apartment building.

"Jeremiah," Asad said.

I turned around.

"I'll see you around?" he said.

I could feel another smile unfurling. "Yeah," I said. "You will."

CHAPTER

"What about this one?" Michael said, pointing to a teal bicycle hanging from the ceiling of the bike shop. "It's a great color. It could be your 'plus-one' at the wedding."

"Ha ha," I said. We were at a real bike shop. Not just a department store that sold cheap bikes. These bikes were meant to last. And there were so many different kinds. They had those recumbent bikes, the kind where you sit back and pedal with your feet up. Cruisers, BMX bikes, mountain bikes, and touring bikes. They even had bicycles that folded up into a square for easy storage and one that was powered by your arms instead of legs. But even here, they had nothing like Michael's Uni-cycle.

Thank God.

I got to take several for spins around the block. I didn't like how the road bikes made me hunch forward over the handlebars. And I definitely wasn't going to go for one of those mini-BMX types. The mountain bikes were a lot more rugged than I needed, especially the ones with the super fat tires.

And then I saw it.

Perfection.

The Titanium Boulevard City Bike. Goldenrod yellow. An oiled leather seat. A rack over the back tire. It was tall for me, but the salesman said that was probably a good thing at my age. It rode as smooth as butter.

I looked at the price tag. "It's really expensive," I said to Dad.

He scratched his chin. "It's really cool, too."

I sighed. "It is."

Dad and Michael looked at each other. Michael raised his eyebrows. Dad gave him cow eyes. Michael sighed, then laughed. "Okay," he said. "But it is coming out of your allowance, Allen."

"How about it comes out of your kombucha budget?" Dad said.

Michael punched him lightly with a laugh.

Dad pulled out his credit card and paid.

The cashier handed over the receipt and said, "We've got a 30-day guarantee. If you don't like it, you can trade it for another model."

"I don't think I'll need to do that," I said. I wasn't going to trade this bike for anything.

"So classy, Jer," Michael said as we rolled it out the door. "It looks like one of those bikes they ride in the Netherlands or Scandinavia.

What are you going to name it?”

I thought for a minute. “I think I’ll go with, ‘The Bicycle.”

“I thought mine was, ‘The Bi-cycle,’ Dad said with a laugh.

“Nice,” I said, rolling my eyes. Dad jokes.

Dad threw my old one into the back of his truck. He said we could drop it off at Goodwill or Salvation Army later. He drove off, and left Michael and I to ride home. Me on the Bicycle, Michael on the Uni-Cycle.

As we rode back towards the apartment, I shifted back and forth between gears, feeling the resistance build with the speed. Eventually, I was way ahead of Michael, whose one speed Uni-Cycle could never keep up. I turned around and rode back to him.

“I still haven’t heard anything from Reina, Lisa, and Sage,” Michael told me.

I switched to a lower gear so I could stay beside him. I thought about the undelivered invitation. I decided to come clean. “I never gave

Sage the invitation."

Michael braked so hard I passed him before I could register that I needed to brake, too. I pulled over to the side and waited for him to roll up to me. I could feel my face getting hot.

"Why?" Michael looked concerned rather than angry.

I tried to think of how to phrase it. "It's just. Sage and Asha are best friends now,"

"Jeremiah," Michael said, understanding in his voice. "You are under no obligation to invite them. We wanted to invite Sage and her moms because we thought you wanted to. But if you don't..."

"I don't know," I said.

A look of realization washed his face and he smacked his forehead. "This is why you've been helping with so much of this wedding stuff," he said. "And I didn't think to ask." Michael sighed. "Why don't you think it over and we decide when we get home?"

I felt childish. Why was it still so hard for me

that Sage had a new friend? I thought about her leaving with Asha to go to swimming classes and I felt a surge of resentment. But then I thought of her texting me. I thought about watching the two of them while standing next to Asad, and some of that resentment fizzled.

Sage was my friend. So were her moms. I was volunteering with Reina all the time. I did want them at the wedding.

"I think I will invite them," I said. "Yeah, I will."

When we got back to the apartment, Sage and Asha were in the park. So was Asad. He looked relieved to see me. He gave me a wave. I waved back. All three of them crossed the street. Michael jerked his head towards them and gave me a look that I figured was supposed to mean, *Give that darn invitation already!* Michael waved at the group as he pulled the Uni-cycle inside.

I dismounted, which was easier next to the

steps due to the extra height.

"Whoa," Asad said. "New bike!"

"Yeah," I said.

"It's the color of sunflowers," Sage said.

"Buttercups," Asha said.

"Mustard," I corrected them.

"It's so… classy," Asad said. I could see something sharp in his eyes: longing or maybe jealousy. I remembered that he and Asha had to share their bike between them, and felt awkward all of a sudden.

"Do you want to give it a spin?" I asked him.

"Can I?" he asked.

I unclipped my helmet and handed it over to him. He was a little taller than I was, so it fit him perfectly. He didn't have to stand on tiptoes. I watched as he rode around the park, clicking through the gears until he soared past.

After several laps, he braked in front of us.

"It's a bird!" Sage said.

"It's a plane!" Asha said.

"It's a Muslim on a bike!" Asad said, and we

all laughed.

Sage wanted to try it, too. She had to stand on the second step of the stoop and have us kind of tilt the bike towards her to get onto it. She could pedal okay once she was up. As she circled the park, I told Asad and Asha that I'd be right back. I ran up the stairs, dug out the rumpled invitation, and slid it into my pocket. I was back to the stoop before Sage pulled up again.

"Wowser," she said as we helped her down. "It rides like yogurt."

"You mean like butter?" I asked, helping her down.

"Butter?" she said. "No. Yogurt. Way sweeter and bright."

"You know what I think?" Asad said. "I think it rides like a bicycle."

I laughed.

Not knowing when I would be able to catch Sage alone, I just handed her the envelope.

"What's this?" she said.

"An invitation," I said. "To Dad and Michael's

wedding." Feeling awkward about not inviting them, I looked at Asha and Asad. I was about to apologize, but neither of them looked bothered.

"Did they all come pre-creased?" Sage laughed, holding up the misshapen envelope.

"No," I said. "Yours is a limited edition stylishly distressed wedding invite."

"Fancy," she said. "And yes, of course we'll be there!"

"You haven't even opened it," I said. "You don't know the date or anything."

"It doesn't matter," Sage said. "We'll be there."

CHAPTER

"What do you want to do?" Asad said.

It was the first time that I'd tracked him down to hang out. Doing this kind of thing still made me nervous. I was the kinda kid who used to hide behind my parents while they arranged the playdates for me when I was little.

But there were no parents to hide behind these

days. Asad seemed cool. Not as a replacement Sage, but just as he was.

So there I was on the front steps of his building.

"We could hang out, I guess," I said. Somehow hanging out on purpose was different than happening to meet up with someone, like at the park or something. "Wanna go for a ride?"

"Sure!" Asad's face lit up. "I've got bike rights today. Where do you want to go?"

"I don't know." I wondered whether I knew about any places he didn't know about. We stared at each other. I was starting to wonder whether this was a good idea after all. I just wasn't good at this. Maybe neither was Asad. "Well..." I said, but didn't know how to complete it.

"I'm gonna take you to my dad's coffee shop," he said.

"Sure," I said, feeling relieved. "Yeah. Let's do it."

We met up a few minutes later, me on my new

bike, Asad on Asha's pink one. He led the way and I followed behind. Where there was room, we rode side by side so we could talk, but talking is difficult when you're pedaling hard.

At a red light, we caught our breath.

"You ever been to a Somali coffee shop?" he asked.

"I'm guessing it's exactly like Starbucks," I said.

He laughed. "Yeah. Exactly."

It was only around a fifteen-minute ride before Asad pointed to a large brick building up ahead. It was a huge tan-brick building maybe ten storeys high. It was old but in a classy way. It had a big central tower that was even taller with a huge sign saying MIDTOWN.

"Come on," Asad said, leading me across Chicago Avenue.

We locked our bikes in front of the building. "This is a pretty big coffee shop," I said. I followed him in to the main floor through doors marked Global Market.

The market was a huge space with cement floors and a tall ceiling. There was row after row of shops and businesses and restaurants.

Asad led the way. We passed a Tibetan shop, a halal grocery store, and a Scandinavian import store.

Asad pointed out highlights to me. "This place has the best lamb you'll ever eat. Ooh. Up here we've got epic tamales. That cheese shop sells little cheese blocks, but stay away from one called Gorgonzola! That's the bubble tea place. Try taro flavored. Uh, that's the medicinal herb place. And," he pointed to a sign that said BULSHADA, "That's Dad's place."

We walked inside. The front was completely open to the rest of the market, but there was still a feeling of it being its own place. Of course, it wasn't like a Starbucks. The light was bright. The walls were covered in posters written in Arabic. Three vining plants grew up strings around the window looking out towards Lake Street. There was a long menu on the wall.

People gathered around the tables and chairs sipping from cardboard cups. Some, I assumed, were Somali. Many of them were not.

Asad pulled me over to the counter, and his dad rose from one of the tables where he had been talking to a group of men leaning in around a newspaper.

"Hello!" he said. "Welcome to Bulshada."

"Thanks," I said.

"Do you know Bulshada?" he asked.

I shook my head.

"The Somali word for Community," his dad said. "Welcome to my community."

"Thanks," I said. It was a pretty great name.

"Now, what would you like?" his dad asked.

"Um," I said. I had no idea what I was supposed to order. I looked at the menu on the wall again, but not all of it was in English. I thought about just ordering a cup of coffee. "I'll try anything," I said.

"Anything?" Asad's dad said. "America. Home of the brave!"

"Not anything," Asad said. "Halwa and Fanta, please."

His dad laughed and sang, "Wanta Fanta. Doncha wanna wanta Fanta." He slid two cans of the orange soda across the counter and selected two large pieces of what looked kind of like dark brown Jell-O®. Or maybe translucent fudge.

"How much?" I asked, pulling out my wallet.

His dad held out his hand. "One thousand dollars," he said, then laughed and waved us off saying it was free for his son and friend. We thanked him and picked a table in the sunlight streaming through the window.

The Fanta was cold and sweet. It felt kind of funny getting such a basic American soda at a Somali coffee shop.

"So Fanta is a type of traditional Somali coffee, huh?" I asked.

"Of course," Asad laughed.

"And what's this brown stuff?"

Asad picked up a piece and took a small bite.

His eyes rolled back in his head. He sucked on the piece, then finally returned to earth. "What is it? It's paradise."

I picked it up. It was soft and gummy. When I bit it, I could see what Asad meant. It tasted deep and rich and spicy and sweet and buttery. "Dang," I said.

Asad laughed. "Right? You're really supposed to drink it with Somali spiced tea, but I prefer it with my trusty Fanta. Sugar and sugar."

We slowly ate our way through the rest of the halwa, then picked up our Fantas, waved to Asad's dad and went back into the maze of the market.

"So there it is," he said. "Dad's coffee shop."

"Fanta shop," I said.

We walked through the shops and past food stands handing out samples. I got to try some of that lamb Asad was such a fan of. I'd never tried lamb before. It practically melted in my mouth and left my mouth glowy with heat. "Lamb is amazing," I said.

Asad laughed and took a sample, too. "Not all lamb," he said. "But their lamb, yes."

While walking through the market with him, I got a memory of going around the Mall of America with Sage and Asha. I looked at Asad and smiled. I followed him through the stalls.

He pointed out the best kinds of Mexican spicy mango candy. I bought one for each of us. "Sugar on sugar on sugar," I said.

He bought us two licorice roots from the herbalist. Not licorice candy. Actual roots.

"What do I do with it?" I asked.

He stuck it into his mouth and rolled it between his molars. "Chew on it. Mother Nature's toothbrush."

"Seriously?" I asked.

"Seriously," he said.

This was a day for trying anything new. I looked at him sideways, but he was chewing away. I tried it. The bark was rough and fibery. The more I chewed it, the sweeter it got. And I could actually feel some of the sugary plaque getting scrubbed away. Or at least I thought I could feel that.

"Is this how Somalis brush their teeth?" I asked.

He busted up laughing. "We typically use toothbrushes. But some of us use licorice root technology."

We laughed together. We walked in and out of the little shops. It was alive. I felt alive in it. I felt alive with him.

When we'd seen the rest of the market, we sat outside in the sun, still chewing the last of our licorice.

"I've been wondering something," I told Asad. I didn't know how to put this, but it was something I'd thought about for a long time. "Are you okay with my family?"

"What do you mean?" Asad said.

I looked straight ahead. "I guess I mean Dad and his boyfriend."

"What about them?" A look of understanding came over Asad's face. "Ah, you mean because they're gay?"

"Well, one of them is," I said. "The other one is bi."

"And Muslims hate gay people?"

"And bi people." I took out my root and inspected its opening fibers. "Don't they?"

"Do Christians hate gay and bi people?" he asked.

I thought about how Dad's parents and my Aunt Paula used the Bible to tell Dad that he and Michael were wrong. Then I thought about Dad and Michael's church where Pastor Veronica preached love and acceptance from the same Bible. "Some do. Some don't."

"Same with Muslims," Asad said. "Islam is crazy huge and full of so many different ideas. Some Muslims think being gay goes against the Quran. And some Muslims fight for gay rights."

"Really? Dang." For some reason I hadn't thought that Islam could be as diverse as Christianity. But of course it would be. No large group is ever only one single thing or idea.

"But to answer your question," Asad said. "Is my family okay with your family? Both of my parents say that being gay or bi or whatever goes against the Quran, but they know your parents aren't Muslim. Why would your parents follow the Quran?"

"Makes sense," I said.

"Do they like it?" Asad asked himself. "Aw, heck no. But that doesn't mean they won't like your dads. Or look at how my parents let Asha take a swimming class with boys and girls. My aunt and uncle in Sweden won't even let their daughters play with boys. Diversity is the spice of society."

I nodded. "That's a good quote. Who said that?"

Asad laughed. "Me."

CHAPTER

At Bridge, we sat cutting pale yellow cardstock into little squares that each had one letter printed on them, kind of like Scrabble tiles. Some of the students were having difficulty cutting the pieces in straight lines.

I sat next to Asli cutting my own set of letters. She finished cutting out the first row, A–J, then looked up at me. “Who are you?” she said.

I stared at her. I’d been sitting next to her for a couple of weeks now. “I’m Jeremiah,” I said. I wondered if she was okay.

“Yes,” she said. “Who are you?”

“Jeremiah,” I repeated.

She shook her head. I wondered if I should call Reina over in case there was something wrong with Asli. Asli’s eyes scanned the ceiling like she was searching for something. I watched her. I was starting to feel nervous.

She made a sound like air escaping from a pump. She tried again. “Who are you doing today?”

It clicked.

Who?

Not who.

How.

“How?” I said. “How are you doing today?”

She squinted at me, then a smile broke across her face. “Who. How.” She started laughing. So did I. Nur and Marner Saw looked at us.

Pretty soon Ifaa and Mustafa were looking, too. Somehow that made it funnier and we just laughed harder.

"Everything okay over there?" Reina asked.

We nodded, laughing harder.

"Who are you?" she repeated. "Who?" When we finally got a hold of ourselves, she said "Not who. How. How are you today?"

"Fine," I said. "Good. I am happy."

"Happy," she said. "Yes. I am happy."

After spelling the vocabulary words with our newly cut letter tiles, and doing an activity where we had to ask each other what we were wearing and use the new descriptive words, we went outside.

The garden was coming along. The tomatoes were in bloom and the beet greens were full enough that we could thin them and send bunches home with some of the students. The carrot and onion tops were growing tall. The beans were flowering. We had some nearly ripe tiny red eggplants that looked more like cherry tomatoes.

Maybe it was the magic of companion planting or the way the students cared for the garden that saturated the place with life.

We took turns hauling the watering cans from the spigot. We had two watering cans now. I had brought the one I got from Mr. Keeler last summer.

Making a garden had been so important to how summer worked last year. This year, it was important, too. But so different. It wasn't me making a garden for someone else. It was all of us growing plants for each other.

CHAPTER

I took my bike out for a spin. It still rode like butter. Or yogurt. So smooth. I rode over to Asad's building to see if he wanted to go for a ride. Asad and Asha were outside on the stoop drinking orange Fanta. I rode up.

"Hey," I said. "Salam alaikum." I had learned this traditional Muslim greeting from Nur and Asli.

"Howdy, partner," Asad replied. "That's the traditional American greeting, right?"

We all laughed.

"Wanna go for a ride?" I asked Asad. I might have asked Asha, too, just to be polite. But they only had the one bike between the two of them.

"Yeah," he said. "Cool. Let me go—"

"Hold it," Asha said. "You promised me that I could have it to ride with Sage today. We're taking a tour of the lakes."

"When?" Asad asked.

"Whenever she gets here," Asha said. "Remember."

Asad shrugged apologetically. "I did promise her."

"Why don't you just ride on the seat behind him," Asha said laughing."

It was then that I remembered.

My old bike! Why had it taken me so long for the obvious to click into place? My old bike was still laying in the back of Dad's truck. Meanwhile, Asad and Asha were still having to trade their bike back and forth.

"Hey," I said. "I have a bike."

"We see that," Asha said.

"No. My old bike. It's in the back of my Dad's truck. You could have it."

Asad's face broke into a smile. "Really?"

"Yeah," I said. "It still works fine."

Sage rode up. "What is everyone looking so happy about?"

"Asad is getting a bike," I said.

"Really? Splendidness!" Sage said.

Asha and Sage took their tour of the lakes.

Since we had to wait for Dad to come home from work in his truck, I locked my bike and Asad and I sat on the front steps of his building and played his Nintendo Switch, passing it back and forth between us. It was pretty old at this point, but it was still fun. We were taking turns playing Mario Kart. Asad did best with Bowser. Oddly enough, I was usually best with Princess Peach, but I didn't typically shout that from the hilltops. I picked Luigi, my second favorite.

I came in third, and handed it back to Asad. He came in first.

When it was closer to the time Dad came home, Asad and I went over to the stoop in front of my building. Dad's truck pulled into the lot and Asad and I explained about the bike. Dad pulled it out of the back.

"Thanks!" Asad said. The bike was short on his legs. Really short. He was taller than me, after all, but he was smiling. As we went for a ride, I had to pedal slower than normal so he could keep up.

"Still," he said. "My own little bike is a lot better than a shared pink one."

CHAPTER 21

Dad came home from work early so he could go with Michael and me downtown for tuxedo fittings. We went down Nicollet to a menswear shop filled with suits, ties, and other boring business clothes. I suddenly felt too casual to be there in my cut-offs and tank top. Michael wore a pink button-up with a pair of designer jeans, but Dad was in his work pants and a Minnesota Wild t-shirt, so I figured I must be okay.

A smiling bald man in a navy blue suit took us to the back of the store where Dad and Michael could look at the different types of tuxedos on the mannequins. They decided to keep it classic with black tuxes. Michael ordered a teal bow tie. Dad picked a brown one the color of a Hershey bar. I decided to go with black.

Getting a tux fitting was a new experience. It was weird having a stranger so close to my body, measuring down my shoulder to my wrist, the inside of my leg, around my waist. As he stretched the measuring tape around my chest, Michael and Dad's phones chimed at the same time.

Michael tapped his screen, his eyes moved back and forth, then he looked up at Dad. "She accepted."

The man jotted down my measurements and Dad stepped up.

"Who accepted?" Dad asked as he stretched out his arm under the measuring tape.

"Paula." Michael scrolled down, then read aloud. "'We think we'll attend your event. RSVP for 9."

"Our *event*," Dad said, sounding kind of hurt and kind of mad. "Event? She can't even call it a wedding. I wonder what she's calling it to her kids. And what are you to them, Michael? Does she talk about you as my roommate?"

The man clicked his tongue and shook his head. "I'm sorry to hear that."

"Sorry," Michael said to the man. "Nothing like dousing you in our drama."

The man laughed. "I do fittings for weddings and prom. Drama is an integral part of my work."

Dad and Michael laughed, but looked at each other in a way that made it obvious that the laughs were to be polite.

"So anyway, all these cousins are coming now," I told Sage, Asha, and Asad. "And I've never met any of them."

"We haven't met our cousins that live in Sweden," Asad said. "Although, according to my mom, they all speak Swedish now, so I probably wouldn't understand them even if we did meet."

Hanging out with Sage and Asha wasn't so weird now that it also included Asad. We were like two teams now, but both playing on the same side.

"Why did you invite them if they don't like gay people?" Sage asked.

"Dad's not gay," I said. "He's bisexual. Dad and Michael thought they should at least *invite* all of their family. My grandparents, aunt, uncle and cousins are all the family we've got."

"The only family you've got?" Sage said. "But are aunt and uncle and cousins really your only family?" Sage said. "I mean, like what defines family?"

"Parents," I said. "Brothers and sisters. Aunts

and uncles. Grandparents. Family."

"I mean, yeah," Sage said. "That's 'family of origin,' but what about family of choice?"

"What is that?" Asha asked. "Like who you marry and stuff?"

Sage shook her head. "It's the people you bring into your life and commit to. Like maybe people in your community. People that you stand by in hard times even if there's no blood connection."

"Like Mr. Keeler," I said.

"Exactly," Sage said. "I think your family of choice is more important than the people you just happen to share DNA with."

I thought about Robi and Em, Sarah, Big Ben and Little Jon, Heather and Dave, Mary and Jo. Michael. Even Sage and her moms. Maybe Sage was right: family of choice *was* more important.

CHAPTER

Working in the garden at Bridge was way more exciting than working on my little plot of stony ground in front of the apartment building. I had planted the alyssum around Mr. Keeler's daylilies which, by now, were in full, fiery bloom. They were bright and alive together.

But at Bridge, there was a different sort of life. I hadn't ever really done vegetable gardening. Sometimes Mom tried to plant a few things, but as I wasn't home over the summer to lend her my green thumb, things went amiss. Mom says she has a brown thumb. Still, she did manage to grow those tomatoes last summer. Everyone can improve.

Every Tuesday I followed the students out to the garden. There was always something in a new stage of growth. The squash was in bloom. The first tiny green beans hung from the bushes.

I expected Robi to take charge, but they typically stood back and let the students take the lead.

"It may sound cliché," Robi said one Tuesday as Marner Saw wove the long tomato stems around another tree branch he'd stuck in the ground. "But jeepers. A good teacher is a devout learner, and I have a lot to learn."

I felt safe and alive in the garden. I think the students did, too.

In late July that all changed.

I followed the class out of the cool dark of the church basement into the glaring July sunshine. Everyone was chattering as we walked along the side of the building to the garden in the back. Even though I hadn't entered the garden yet, I was already smiling.

I joined the line next to Robi. They smiled at me. "Are you ready for some serious watering?" they asked. "These last few days have been—"

I heard a sort of cry from the front of the line. Everyone hurried forward. The students had formed a silent ring around the edge of the garden. I found a gap where I could see what they were looking at.

The garden was destroyed.

Someone had pulled out the tomatoes. Smashed the zucchini. Slashed the eggplant and cabbages. Uprooted the lemongrass.

But that wasn't even the worst of it. Whoever had demolished the garden had also spray-painted the brick wall of the church:

YOU DON'T BELONG HERE
STAY AWAY

The silence was broken by murmurs from the higher-level students interpreting the sign for the beginning students.

I had the sudden impulse to jump in front of the vandalism. To hide it like it was something indecent. Which it was.

But there was no hiding it. We all stood, stunned.

It was only when I felt something wet drip down my face that I realized I was crying. Not because I was sad. Or not only because I was sad. The surging emotion inside me was anger. Who would do this? I wanted to meet them. To punch them. To smash their face into that repulsive message.

Asli was the first to move. She bent down. She knelt in front of the raised bed, picked up half a green watermelon, flecked with dirt. She stood and carried it to the compost. "Clean up," she said.

"Clean up," several others repeated.

We all got to work in silent slow-motion clearing out the destroyed plants and carefully supporting any that had any chance of survival.

Taban, the teacher of the higher-level class, sorted out any vegetables that could still be eaten from the pile of smashed produce.

Robi organized us into groups. Some of us gently replanted everything that had been uprooted. Others watered the traumatized plants.

Reina called Lisa. Lisa showed up still in her uniform from Marzetti's hardware with several large bottles of something called *Graffiti Blaster.* She sprayed it on the bricks and, slowly, the paint started to bubble and turn soft and stretchy. She only sprayed some of the letters, leaving big chunks of the message untouched. She took a wire brush and started scrubbing the disintegrating paint out of the bricks.

Robi went inside and came back with the packs of seeds from the beginning of the year. We replanted in the empty spaces. Maybe it was too late for these seeds to turn into something. But maybe not.

We took turns with the watering cans.

When we'd finished, the garden still looked bleak. Like someone whose hair was cut off in random chunks.

We went back inside. The students packed up their things and left. I pushed in the chairs and wiped the board.

"What if those people come back?" I asked Reina.

She shook her head and gritted her teeth. "Then we clear and replant."

I followed her outside. We walked back to where Lisa was finishing with the graffiti.

"What do you think?" Lisa called.

Simply by eliminating letters, the wall now read:

YOU DO BELONG HERE
STAY

Later when Dad and I rode around the Lake

of the Isles, I was still thinking about the graffiti. When we took a water break, I told him what had happened.

"I'm pissed," I said.

Dad reached out and gripped my shoulder. "You should be."

"Why would someone do that?"

Dad and I looked out over the water. We watched someone kayak past and automatically raised our hands in a wave.

"I don't know," Dad finally said. "Hate is a complicated thing. Whether it's hate towards family or queer people or refugees or Muslims. If there's one thing I've noticed about hate, it's that it usually comes from people who are afraid."

"Afraid?" I didn't see how that made any sense.

Dad sighed. "Afraid of new ideas or unknown people or religions or other differences. People get scared and do terrible things."

"Like your parents?" I asked. "Or Aunt Paula?"

"I think so," he said. "I think that somewhere inside, they're just scared and don't know what to do with that fear."

"But that doesn't make it okay," I said.

"No," Dad said. We remounted our bikes. "It definitely does not make it okay."

CHAPTER 23

The sun was out, but so were the clouds, in the way that makes the day warm and cool all at once. Just when the light gets to be too much, a cloud hurries in to cool you off again. The unnamed clouds made me miss Sage and last summer. But things change. Sage was with Asha at the Y, doing free swim.

I sat in the park with Asad, and I was happy to be with him, passing his Nintendo Switch back and forth while we talked about random stuff.

Eventually, I told him about the graffiti at Bridge. "Can you believe that?" I said at the end of the story.

He was quiet while he finished the final lap as Bowser. When he crossed the finish line he handed me the Switch.

"Yeah," he said. "I can believe it. I wish that was the first time someone did or said something like that. I've had kids at school say stuff like that to me."

"What?" I said. "Seriously?"

He stared straight ahead. "Yeah."

"Dang." I set the Switch on the grass between us. "How do you deal with that?"

"I don't know," Asad said. "Sometimes people suck. But you have to know who you are and just move on."

"I don't know if I could," I said.

"Me neither." Asad laughed. "Maybe we'll

get better with practice, but hopefully all this practice will be able to stop."

He handed me the controller again. I assumed that meant he was ready to move on from the conversation.

"Okay," I said. "Get ready to watch me lose again."

"Don't feel bad," Asad said. "There is nothing you can do about it. I was born with the skills to rule."

I punched his arm and we both laughed.

"Seriously, though," he said. "I have a Nintendo at home, too. An N64. So my skills are crazy good."

That was some serious vintage. I was a little jealous.

"Wanna see it?" he said. He seemed happy to be done with the graffiti conversation. I was too.

"Sure," I said.

He got up and led the way across the park. I hadn't been to his apartment. Somehow going there felt significant. It was his private domain.

The front door of his building was propped open with a brick, so he didn't need a key. His building was another one of these old apartment buildings with big windows and wood trim. I assumed it would look like the inside of Dad and Michael's building. But it had obviously been remodeled at some point. The heavy woodwork had been replaced by bright white walls and burgundy carpet. I followed Asad down the front stairs to a little downstairs lobby with a plastic plant and the apartment mailboxes.

He opened a door across from the mailboxes.

"Here we are," he said. "Home sweet home."

He kicked off his shoes and stepped inside. I followed, kicking off my own. He dropped them into a big plastic tub inside the door.

The living room/dining room was spacious and clean. The apartment was on garden level, which meant the windows were just above the level of the ground outside. It made the apartment feel a little like it was right next door to a conservatory. This feeling was even stronger from the collection of vining plants that grew on strings, stretching across the wall up towards the light of the window.

There was a large map of the world on the wall and three brass clocks all showing different times.

His mom was sitting at a small table. Textbooks and an open laptop surrounded her. She looked up from what I could tell was algebra. I remembered they had said she was working for her GED, which is like a high school diploma.

She looked somehow different to me, but I couldn't put my finger on it. It was only when she'd picked up her hijab from the back of her chair, that I realized that was what had looked different. Her hair. She pulled the hijab over her head. Somehow, I had assumed she just wore her hijab all the time.

"Hello," she said. "How are you?"

"Good," I said. "Salaam alaikum."

She smiled big. "Wa 'alaikum salam. You are hungry?"

I shrugged.

Asad said, "Yes."

She went to the kitchen.

"What's with the clocks?" I asked.

"Three time zones," Asad said and pointed to each one. "Minnesota. Borlange, Sweden where my aunt and uncle live. The Dadaab refugee camp where my uncle and grandparents live. That way we don't call them in the middle of the night."

"Good thinking," I said.

"Come on." Asad led me to the living room. There was a big fluffy couch against the wall across from a large flat-screen TV. The floor was covered with a large red and gold rug and a collection of pillows and cushions. Asad pulled two cushions over for us to sit on in front of their TV. While Asad hooked up the N64, his mom came back with a plate of cookies and two cans of Fanta. It was room temperature, but I didn't mind. Staying with Michael, I didn't get much soda.

"Adaa mudan!" I said, feeling pretty proud of myself. More words I'd picked up from Asli and Nur.

Asad and his mom started laughing. Not mean laughing. Just laughing.

"What?" I said.

"You just said, 'You're welcome,'" Asad said.

"Dang it," I said, wracking my brain for the right one. "Mahadsanid?" I tried again.

"That's the one," Asad said.

"Good, good!" his mom said. "Adaa mudan."

Still chuckling, she went back to her homework.

My cheeks were kinda hot. But honestly, volunteering at Bridge meant that I'd had a lot more practice making a fool of myself.

Asad handed me one controller, and took the other. Pretty soon we were too far into *Super Smash Bros.* to notice whether or not I'd said the wrong thing. Asad was wicked good as Jigglypuff. I kept switching between characters hoping that Mario, Yoshi, or Fox might be my ticket to success.

Eventually we moved on to *The Legend of Zelda™: Ocarina of Time*, passing the controller back and forth every time we died. Apparently Zelda was the one game he hadn't mastered.

"How did you get this thing?" I asked. N64s were worth a lot of money, especially for a collection with so many games.

"My older brother," Asad said. "He had it for years. He's 28 now."

Whoa. That was old for a brother. He could almost be our dad. After giving up on the water temple in Zelda, we landed on *Super Smash Bros* again.

The door to the apartment opened. Asad's dad came in, his deep voice booming out a greeting. His mom rose to greet him, and I shook his hand, saying the greeting correctly. I half wanted him to give me something just so I could use *Thank you* and *You're Welcome* correctly. He wore a hat that lay close to his head, and a brown sports jacket. It seemed awfully warm for something like that.

He came over and watched us fighting: Donkey Kong vs Mario.

"Fighting daanyeer," his dad said. "*America. Home of the brave.*" He laughed then walked away.

"That's his favorite phrase in English," Asad said.

"I was starting to see that," I said. "It's a good one. A classic." I smashed Mario off the platform. "What's daanyeer?"

"Donkey Kong," Asad said. "More or less."

I laughed. "Home of the brave."

CHAPTER

24

"Two weeks!" Michael shrieked when he looked at the calendar on his phone.

I wasn't sure whether it was a happy or terrified yell. It was probably both.

"Two weeks," Dad said, coming into the living room, He scooted a pile of boxes of those teal jars out of the way and came around behind Michael. "Two weeks until you're mine." He threw back his head and did a cheesy, evil villain laugh. "Mwahahaha."

Michael tilted his head back to look back at Dad. "I already am yours."

Dad bent down and kissed him.

"Come on, guys," I said. "Not in front of the kids."

"Feel free to leave," Dad said, his eyes twinkling.

I was actually about to leave anyways. I had an afternoon of volunteering ahead of me at Bridge. Usually I just did the mornings, but today they had just received a load of coats, boots, and other essentials. It was still pretty early in the year for donations like that, but according to Reina they could never have too much winter gear on hand. And it was sometimes easier to get winter donations during the spring and summer when people were cleaning out closets or getting ready to buy all their back-to-school stuff.

"Two weeks, though," Michael said. He ran his fingers through his hair. "That's not enough time to—"

"It's enough time," Dad said, starting to massage Michael's shoulders. "Everything will work itself out."

Michael gave an exasperated sigh. "You know when you say that, what it actually means is, 'Michael will work everything out,' right?"

"Let me help, then," Dad said. "Stop being a bridezilla."

I couldn't help but laugh, but still, I wasn't surprised by what came next.

"Whoa," Michael said. He stood up, pulling away from Dad's hands. "Crossed a line, there Al."

I could tell he was really mad because he called Dad Al.

Dad bit his lip. I could tell that he was working hard not to smile. "Sorry, babe," he finally said, making his face turn serious.

Michael tightened up and looked like he

was searching for something really intense to say back. But he finally relaxed his shoulders. "Sometimes it is harder to share a task than just do it myself. I really appreciate that you booked everything for the honeymoon."

Dad looked sideways. "Booked? I planned where we were going. I don't think we need to book anything. We'll just find places to stay."

Michael's eyes got huge. "Are you serious?"

"Uhhhhh," Dad said. "What I meant is that when I get back from the job this afternoon, I am going to go online and make phone calls and get that all lined up for you?"

"You'd better," Michael said.

Dad pulled Michael towards him. "I will."

Michael melted a little. "Thank you." He leaned in towards Dad for a kiss.

I took that as my cue. "Bye!" I called and hurried into the hall.

———

At Bridge, I found Reina and Lisa standing in the middle of a mountain range of boxes and plastic bags in the basement. Lisa wore a pair of overalls. Reina was in jeans rather than her typical dress. They looked ready to work.

And then a head popped up from the mountain. Sage. Her hair was pulled back under a tie-dye bandana.

"Jeremiah!" Sage called to me.

"Oh," I said. "Hi."

"The fun has arrived!" Sage said to me. I wasn't sure if she meant me or all the stuff.

"Here's the deal," Reina said. "We've got four tables: one for clothes, one for boots, one for coats, and one for all the miscellaneous stuff: hats, scarves, gloves. We can put the garbage pile over by the door. Dust masks on."

"You're here," I said to Sage as she handed me a dust mask. I pulled it over my ears. Even after the past month and a half, I still wasn't exactly sure how I felt about hanging out with Sage.

"I love sorting days," Sage said, her voice muffled behind her mask. "They're like

Christmas!"

Sage tore open a black garbage bag full of boots. I helped her find the pairs and line them up across the folding table.

"What's the garbage pile for?" I asked.

"Excellent question," Reina said. She dug down into a paper bag and pulled out a white ski jacket. She held it up. It was stained with what looked like coffee. There was a jagged tear down the front, spilling the fluffy insulation.

"How about this?" Sage held up a pair of fur-topped boots. She turned them upside down and I could see that the rubber soles were cracked and the heels worn all the way through.

"Check out these babies," Lisa said, displaying a pair of those "magic" gloves. Every finger except the pinkies were frayed open at the tips.

I watched as Sage threw the worn-out boots through the air at the slowly growing garbage pile.

"Every year," Reina said, "We get these bags

of people's old stuff. Sometimes we get new items, but for the most part, the donations are used. Some of it is just used, outgrown, or out of style. Some of it isn't usable any more. Still, people feel like they did something to save these poor, poor refugees from having nothing." She laid out a parka on the coat table. "Our refugee neighbors are not beggars who need to be saved. But some of them do need help."

Lisa held up another pair of cracked boots. "Do our neighbors deserve boots that will fall off their feet? Or a coat that will let the wind right in to beat against their chest?"

"But what happens if you don't have enough?" I said.

"We scramble for more donations," Reina said. "We write grants asking for funds from corporations that want to make a tax-deductible donation. We pull what we need together somehow. Trash should go to the dump, not to our neighbors and friends."

Lisa nodded. "If we expect others to

be grateful to accept our garbage, that's a problem."

That made sense. It made a lot of sense. I thought uncomfortably about how just that spring, Mom had given me a bag and told me to go through my closet to find any clothes that I'd outgrown to give to the homeless shelter downtown. Now I remembered that many of the shirts were really worn out. At least two of them had holes in the armpits. I'd even thrown in a pair of sneakers that had started to split down the side of each foot. And I had felt really good about it. Helping the less fortunate.

I opened a bag and pulled out a pile of what looked like brand new, hand-crocheted hats, mittens, gloves, and scarves.

Reina tore open a blue trash bag stuffed with wadded-up ponchos, the plastic kind that are supposed to be disposable. They were all different colors. Blue, yellow, safety green, pink, orange. "These should keep people warm this winter," she laughed. She dug into the bag.

"There's a gazillion of them."

"Make that two gazillion," Lisa said, holding up another blue trash bag.

"Who knows?" Reina said. "Maybe they'll come in useful for something." She grabbed both bags and carried them to the miscellaneous table.

I opened a bag and found three new coats, tags still on them.

"Jackpot!" Sage yelled.

I laid them out on the coat table. The next bag was full of mittens. All of them used. I matched them together. There were two mismatched left hands.

Was it better to have one warm hand than two cold ones? One of them had a tear at the base of the thumb. The other looked mostly okay. Faded, but in one piece. I double checked for a match for either of them. No luck.

I made a mental note to tell Dad and Michael that they should buy some gear to donate. I looked at the mittens for a good minute, then brought them both to the trash pile.

By the end of the sorting, Sage and I were laughing over the strange donations and having fun with the work. I was having fun with her. We were having fun together. We were still friends. Maybe not best friends anymore, but friends.

———

Later that day, I met up with Asad for a ride to his dad's coffee shop. Asad rode ahead of me on the sidewalk along Franklin Avenue I watched the way his knees bent up way past his waist as he rode.

The bike was absolutely too small for him. It was too small for me and I was shorter than he was. I had felt so good when I gave him that bicycle. Like I was doing something totally awesome for him.

He stood up on the pedals to make it up the hill. He had to bend over a lot to keep hold of the handlebars.

It didn't fit.

It didn't fit him at all.

I stood on the pedals of my own bike that I was still growing into. That I had room to grow into. I thought again about the sorting at Bridge. I didn't feel so great about my gift anymore.

CHAPTER

"Do you still have the receipt for my bike?" I asked while Michael was making supper. Dad was home, but he was showering off a layer of dirt.

Michael was concentrating on the seared jackfruit barbecue in front of him.

"The receipt," I repeated. "Hello?"

He looked up at me. “What receipt?”

“For my bike.”

Michael took a pair of tongs and started scooping the shredded jackfruit out of the frying pan into a bowl of sauce. “Receipt. Bicycle. Yes. Yes, they emailed me a copy. Why? Do you need to return it? Did you plummet into another pothole?”

“Yeah,” I said. “The entire frame is shot, and I don’t even know where the handlebars landed.”

Michael froze and stared in horror at me, then broke out laughing as he realized I was being sarcastic.

“So, what’s this all about?” he asked as he collected himself.

“I want to return it.”

Dad walked in and pinched a snitch of barbecue from the bowl. “Dang! You know how to cook,” he said.

“Jeremiah wants to return his bike,” Michael said.

“I thought it was the bike of your dreams,”

Dad said.

I sighed. “It is. Or it was.”

Michael cocked his head. “And you want to return it?”

“Kinda,” I said. “I know it was really expensive. I was hoping to exchange it. For two bicycles.”

Dad raised his eyebrows. “Two?”

“For a back-up when you fall into potholes?” Michael said.

“For me and Asad.”

And suddenly I was telling them about how Asad and Asha had been sharing bikes. I told them about how I'd given the old, small bike to Asad, even though he was taller than I was. I told them about helping sort the donations at Bridge. About the boots with holes in them. And the tattered mittens with no right hands.

“I don't need a crazy fancy bike,” I said. “And Asad doesn't need one that's too small for him.”

Dad and Michael looked at each other.

Michael raised his eyebrows. Dad shrugged. Michael nodded.

"You're really growing up, Jer," Dad said. "I think that's a great idea. If that's what you want to do, we'll do it."

I felt a smile rise up in me. "Awesome," I said.

"Hold up," Michael said. "You still have someone else to ask, if you haven't already."

"Who?" I asked.

"Asad," Michael said. "It isn't really our choice to decide what is going to be best for him."

"Oh," I said. "Oh yeah."

Sometimes it felt a little complicated being respectful. A little more work. But I was starting to understand it was worth it.

It turned out that Asad happened to be 100% on board with the idea.

"But seriously, are you sure?" he asked. "This was The Bike of Wonder. The Bike of Dreams. Lightning fast. Smooth as yogurt. And all those baskets."

It was true. My mustard-yellow Titanium Boulevard City Bike. I couldn't deny that a part of me felt really bummed to see it go. But another part of me, at least as strong, just felt happy. It felt right.

"I'm sure," I said.

After his parents approved the plan, Asad brought out a jar of money and handed it to me. The money he'd been saving for his bike.

"You don't have to," I said.

"Neither do you," he said.

"Okay," I said.

Dad drove us to the bike shop in Uptown later that evening. Michael had to stay behind because there was only enough room for three in Dad's truck, and also because he was spraying a clear coat of shellac over the teal and chocolate napkin rings. Asad and I brought our helmets along so we could ride home.

When we got to the shop, Dad talked with the tattoo-covered sales clerk while Asad and I looked at the bikes.

"We should get matching tricycles," he said, pointing to the adult-sized trikes with big baskets in the back. "We could put groceries, or even our parents, in baskets that big."

I tried to picture Asad's dad folded into the back. Probably saying, *America. Home of the brave*. I laughed.

"How about a tandem?" I said.

Asad laughed. "Perfect. But not to ride together. Just to ride on our own. Are you sure you don't need the glittery pink with streamers? You could make your own Uni-cycle."

Laughing aside, we finally picked matching hybrids. The kind that can handle both city riding and a little off road adventure once in a while. They didn't have baskets, but they did have racks on the back for transporting stuff. I knew Dad could give us some bungee cords. We could at least strap on a backpack or something.

They were the same make and model, but Asad's was emerald green and mine was ruby red. Or ketchup and pickle relish, as Asad pointed out. The perfect follow-up to a mustard bike.

Between Asad's money and returning the other bike, we had just enough for our two new ones.

On the way home, we rode side by side. Neither of us had to be the leader. Neither of us had to trail behind. It was better together.

CHAPTER

It was the week of the wedding.

Finally.

Even though it was only Monday, Michael was checking his weather app every couple of hours for the Saturday forecast. A weather forecast can change a lot, even in the span of 24 hours, in Minnesota. But there was a pesky 30% chance of rain that kept hanging over the end of the week.

"It can't rain," Michael said.

"It won't rain," Dad said.

Whether or not it rained, they had the pavilion at Powderhorn Park, so the ceremony could be held inside where the reception was going to be. I didn't see why it was such a big deal. But of course, Michael thought everything was a big deal.

I sat at our apartment table sliding slips with names printed on them into the little silver frames. They were to show where everybody was supposed to sit. Eight to a table, except of course where cousin Paula and her family would squeeze in a ninth.

I didn't recognize all of the names, but most of them were familiar to me. Friends from cocktail hour, a few people that worked at Real Foods with Michael. I recognized several of the names from Michael's family tree. Even though he'd made me go through it another two times during the summer, I couldn't place faces with the names in my head.

Michael sat beside me, precisely clipping the name slips down to size. "Maybe hand-lettered calligraphy was a bit much for these," he said. "Do you think I should've gone more minimalist? I could've just printed them. Maybe Helvetica would've been a good font."

Dad walked into the room, his cell phone in hand.

"How's it going, babe?" Michael asked.

Dad gave half a shrug. "Well, that drama with Paula is over at long last."

"What do you mean?" Michael asked. "I just submitted the final number to the caterer. Please don't tell me—"

"They're not coming," Dad said.

"No," Michael said. "Did she say why?"

"She said she couldn't 'condone' our relationship to her kids. She said they would still come if they could skip our 'unholy' ceremony." Dad gave a little laugh. I could tell it hurt, though. "I told her not to bother. She and her family are no longer invited."

"Just like that?" Michael said.

"Just like that," Dad said.

"Oh Allen," Michael said. "None of your family will be here?"

"My family is here," Dad said. "You and Jer. Our community. Our friends. That's my family."

Michael stood up and wrapped his arms around Dad. "Dang, girl," Michael said. "You tell 'em! Who needs Paula or your parents? They're dead to me!"

Dad laughed, pulling Michael close. "I wasn't going to be that dramatic."

I sighed. "You could've uninvited her before I hand-lettered all nine name thingies."

Dad and Michael laughed.

"Well," Michael said. "We've got nine extra spots. Anybody else who needs to come? What about the guys who operate the other big machines you work with? Construction workers always spice things up."

“I think I’ll bring enough construction spice,” Dad said.

“Well, we’re already paying,” Michael said.

“Maybe I could invite Asad,” I cut in. Dad and Michael both looked at me.

“It’s worth a try,” Michael said. Then his face broke into a smile. “Yes. Yes, you should. What about his family?”

“Asha.” I nodded. “And maybe their parents.” I was counting on my fingers now. “And Asli, and Mustafa. Marner Saw. Ifaa and Nur?”

Dad gripped my shoulder. “I think that’s a great idea.”

We packed all of the decorations, bars of soap, teal tinted jars, name plates, and all of that into large plastic totes and piled the doily globes on top of the lot.

I was ready to bid all of it farewell. As I balanced the last doily globe onto the pile, I realized the wedding also meant my summer was coming to an end.

Dad and Michael were going for a honeymoon on a "national parks whirlwind," as Michael put it. Mount Rushmore, the Grand Tetons, Yellowstone, Glacier, Sequoia, Yosemite. If it was going to be a whirlwind, it was going to be a very slow one that involved weeks of driving. Dad had finally booked all the places they were going to stay and Michael said he was a miracle worker and kissed him. There was too much kissing happening around here these days.

Originally, they had talked about waiting for the honeymoon until I moved back with Mom, but returning to Iowa after the wedding only cut two weeks off my summer in Minneapolis. And I had said that it was fine. They should go ahead. It was their honeymoon after all.

Now that it was almost time for me to go back to Iowa, losing those two weeks felt like I would be missing a lot.

CHAPTER

27

I was about to leave.

Leave Asad.

And Bridge. Dang, was I going to miss Bridge. I was going to miss the garden that we'd finally gotten in order again. The good morning routine. The students and all their quirky habits. Asli, Nur, Ifaa, Marner Saw, Mustafa.

Even the thought of leaving Sage and Asha made me feel low.

All of a sudden, I realized that this was my last day volunteering at Bridge. I had a handful of wedding invitations. They weren't the ones that had been professionally printed at the beginning of the summer, but Michael made them look pretty good on his laptop before printing them.

"*Who* are you?" Asli said with a laugh as she sat down next to me.

I smiled. "I am good. *Who* are you?"

"Very good," she said.

When class started, Reina didn't immediately go into the morning routine.

"Good morning," she said.

"Good morning," we all said back to her.

"Today is Jeremiah's last day." She paused. Several students looked at me, squinting their eyes in thought.

"Last day?" Nur said.

"Yeah," I said.

Nur nodded.

Asli said, "Next week, no Jeremiah?"

"Yeah," I said.

I got a jumble of goodbyes.

I stood up with the envelopes, passing them around the circle. "On Saturday, my dad is getting married." I held up an extra copy of the invitation.

"Married," Reina repeated. She clicked through pictures of weddings from their cultures and other cultures around the world.

Marner Saw looked up from his dictionary. "Wedding," he said.

"Yes," Reina nodded. "A wedding."

Everybody nodded.

She showed a picture of a wedding with a man and a woman standing at an altar in front of a suited man with a stained-glass window in the background.

"Wedding," she said.

"Wedding," the class repeated.

Then she pulled up a picture of two women getting married. It took me a minute to realize it was her wedding photo; she and Lisa radiated happiness.

"Wedding," Reina said.

"Yes," Marner Saw said. "Wedding."

Asli squinted at the screen. "Teacher wedding," she said, nodding. "Woman and woman."

Nur was shaking his head.

Then Reina pulled up a picture of two men in tuxes standing hand in hand. "Wedding," she said.

"Man and man," Nur said. "Woman and woman. I don't like."

"I know this," Ifaa said. "Gay. Lesbian. Gay men. Lesbian women."

Reina nodded. "Gay. Lesbian."

I mean, Dad wasn't gay, but it did simplify things. I was starting to wonder whether inviting was a good idea. So far the responses hadn't been the best to the pictures of same-sex weddings.

"My father and his boyfriend are getting

married," I said.

"Your father," Marner Saw said, "is getting married."

"Yes," I said. "To another man."

I waited a few minutes.

"Two men." I pointed to the picture.

"Two men," Asli said. "Father and father?"

I nodded.

"Ah," Ifaa said. "Yes. It's different. Different from my culture."

I handed out the invitations. We took a minute for everyone to look them over and process, then Reina wrote the date and time of the wedding on the board.

"Will you come?" I asked.

Several of the students looked at one another. Reina said she would drive the van.

"Man and man," Asli said. She gave a nervous laugh. "I don't like man and man. Woman and woman. America is different."

"I will go," Mustafa said.

I gave him a smile of gratitude.

"Man and man," Nur said. "Woman and woman. I don't like," he echoed Asli.

"I don't like man and man," Asli said again. "I do like Jeremiah. Yes. I will go."

Ifaa's crooked smile broke over his face. "I will go. Yes. Very different."

Marner Saw nodded. "Different is okay."

"Different is good," Ifaa said. "America."

All four of them looked at Nur. He threw up his hands. "Okay," he said. "Okay. Yes."

For some reason, we all started laughing. I felt warm all over inside.

"Okay," Reina said, finally. "What is the date today?"

After class, it looked like it was going to rain. Reina sent me to a closet where I pulled out the bag of donated ponchos. We handed out big handfuls to the students.

"Some for you," I said. "Some for your families." By the time all the students in both classes had taken large bunches of them, we only had a few left.

When I said my last goodbye, I went behind the church to check on the garden. More plants than I had expected survived. We still had several tomatoes, their fruit ripening to a deep red. One of the cantaloupes grew up the branch that Marner Saw stuck into the ground. A bunch of beets that had been flattened had already pushed up new green leaves.

I looked up at what was left of the graffiti again.

YOU BELONG HERE
STAY

I looked at the plants. Things were always stronger than I expected them to be. Able to grow through so much.

CHAPTER

That afternoon, I found Asad sitting in the park with Asha and Sage. They all waved and I went over to join them.

We all laid on our backs, looking up at the sky. Clouds drifted by against the blue. I thought about the beginning of the summer and how I was so afraid of losing Sage and so annoyed with Asha.

Now here we all were, Asad, Sage, Asha and I. Things felt different. Easier. When you're not trying to prove something or grip so tight, you can start to enjoy things for what they are instead of what you expect them to be.

"Watch this." Asha pulled Sage to her feet. Asad and I sat up to watch them. The two of them did coordinated cartwheels, then Sage did a handstand while Asha climbed on top of the picnic table and did a flip off of it.

"And now for the grand finale," Sage yelled. She and Asha both tucked themselves in and started somersaulting down the hill. They crashed into each other halfway down, their somersaults bursting like popcorn. They busted up laughing. So did Asad and I. We clapped while they pulled each other to their feet and took a bow.

They were a lot more fun to watch when I wasn't the only one in the audience. When I was sitting next to a friend.

"I've got something for you two," I said. "I'll

be right back."

I brought down the invitation Michael had printed, and I asked Asad and Asha whether their family wanted to come to the wedding.

"Seriously?" Asad asked. "Wow. I've never been to a white-people wedding. It will be interesting to learn about your exotic culture."

"The wedding might not be too traditional," I said.

"I don't know," Asha said. "If this is the first white wedding, it is the standard by which all white weddings shall be judged henceforth."

They promised to ask their parents.

"We'll all be there then," Sage said, beaming.

I found that I was smiling at the idea. "Yeah," I said. "I hope so."

"What's a gay wedding like?" Asha asked.

"Like any other wedding, I guess," I said.

"Any other wedding?" Asha laughed. "Why? Are all weddings pretty much the same? Who wears the henna in a gay wedding?"

"I don't know," I said. I wasn't even sure what

henna was. Honestly, I hadn't even been to many weddings. I didn't know whether or not Dad and Michael's wedding was going to be "normal."

Normal. That word.

"Neither of my moms wore henna when they got married," Sage said. "But I got to be a flower girl in the sparkliest dress I could find."

"Aw. So cute," Asha said. "Little Sage in a glittery dress. I bet you were adorable. When did your moms get married?"

"Two years ago," Sage said with a laugh.

"I get to be the flower girl at Dad and Michael's wedding," I said. "They even got me a pink dress to match the little basket."

Asha busted out laughing. Her laughter was so bright and bold, I couldn't not laugh with her. Pretty soon all of us were laughing. Together.

We lay in the sunshine a while longer until Sage sat up. "I'm melting," she said, fanning her face with her hands.

"Melting?" Asha said. "I'm already melted."

I took off my *ALLY* hat to wipe the sweat off

my forehead. I looked at Asha in her hijab. "No wonder you're melting," I said. "Doesn't it suck to have to wear a hijab all summer?"

"*Have* to wear a hijab?" Asha said.

I could feel my face getting a little hotter. "I mean, don't you?"

She considered. "Do you *have* to wear your Ally hat?" she said, pointing to the hat Michael had bought me at Pride last summer.

"No," I said.

"But you do," she said. "Why?"

I thought for a minute. "I like it. I guess it shows other people a little bit of who I am."

"Like it's a piece of what you believe?" Asha asked.

"Yeah," I said.

"I *get* to wear my hijab kind of like that," Asha said.

"Oh." I had never thought about it like that.

"Okay," Sage said. "Jeremiah is less ignorant now." Everyone laughed. Even me. "Now how about a trip to the pool? You two should come."

Sage pointed to Asad and I.

"Pwetty pwease," Asha said, putting on a big pout.

"How could you say no to that?" Asad turned to me. "What do you think?"

"Yeah," I said. "Okay. Let's do it."

We met up on our bikes since each of us had our own bike now. Sage and Asha led the way. Asad and I rode behind.

In the locker room at the Y, Asad and I were already in our swim trunks, so we just took off our shirts and stashed them in a locker. Asad's swimsuit covered his belly button and fell below his knees. For some reason when I pulled off my shirt, I felt awkward with how much of my knees and stomach were exposed, but Asad didn't seem to notice. He led the way to the pool.

The pool was large. It had areas roped off for people swimming laps, but a bunch of other kids and adults were in the open swimming area. Asad did a cannonball into the pool, and a lifeguard yelled at him.

"Sorry," he called to the lifeguard. He swam towards me with a huge smile on his face. "Worth it," he said.

I climbed the ladder down into the cool water.

Sage and Asha emerged. Sage wore a sequined bikini. Asha wore her burkini. It was silvery green with almost as many sequins as Sage's, though in swirls rather than solid. The material covered her arms and legs and went up around her head, kinda like a snug hijab. They were right. It did make her look like a mermaid. Maybe part mermaid and part Olympic swimmer.

She wasn't the only one in a burkini, but still, I noticed people staring at her like she was doing something weird. Not everyone. But some people. I wanted to make them stop. I wondered whether I might have done that if I didn't know her. I hoped not.

She must have noticed me staring back at the people who were staring at her.

"Yes," she said. "Some people stare. Welcome to my life."

"They're just jealous," Sage said.

"They're just ignorant," I said, happy to feel like I wasn't the one doing something stupid.

Asha and Asad laughed. "They're just both."

"Ignore them," Asha said. "All eyes on me. Check out this expert, Olympic-level doggy paddle."

CHAPTER

The Red Hot Art Festival was in full swing across the street in the park. Tents, booths, and food trucks filled the small space. It was nothing compared to the size of Pride or the Uptown Art Fest, but it was still cool. Sage, Asad, Asha and I had walked through the booths. The art here wasn't as fancy or epic as the Uptown festival. More like it had been made by normal people. Not that artists aren't normal.

But I mean, this festival was just quirkier. For instance, there were giant cardboard boxes with artists inside. They would make a work, then stand up in their box and walk it to a new spot, leaving the freshly made work behind. If you liked it, you could buy it for any price, slipping the money in through a little hole in their box.

Asha slipped five dollars into a box in exchange for a painting of two lady bugs with boxing gloves in a fight.

"It's just so inspiring," Asha said.

"It's gonna beat out the Mona Lisa," Sage said. "Instead of people wondering why old Mona is smiling, they can wonder what in the heck these ladybugs are doing in a fight."

"Probably just cardio," I said.

We all bought some mini-donuts. We didn't linger too long, though. My phone buzzed. According to the text, Mom was going to be there any minute now.

My friends followed me back to the stoop.

“What does she look like?” Sage said. “You look so much like your Dad, that I kinda always assumed that if you look like you mom, too, she must look like your Dad.”

“Logic,” Asha said. “Does your mom have messy brown hair and a beard?’

“Shut up,” I laughed. “She’s a little taller than me. Her hair is straight like mine, but blond. Well, it’s naturally blond, but she dyes it a lot.” That spring it had been purple with periwinkle highlights. I wondered what it would look like now. If she’d done anything with it for the wedding.

“I wish I could dye my hair,” Sage said. “But dying black hair takes a few more steps. I’ll probably go pink sometime.”

“Yes, please!” Asha said.

Finally, a gold Ford pulled up. I could see Mr. Wirtz with his balding head and clear-framed glasses. “Jeremiah!” he called out.

The passenger side door opened and Mom ran around the front of the vehicle to me, arms open. It had only been two months since I'd last seen her, but it always felt strange to see her again at the end of the summer. She always looked a little older, like she did all of her aging during the summertime.

This year, though, she didn't look any older. The lines at the edges of her eyes were still there, but her eyes were opened wide. Her eyebrows had a light lift to them.

She looked really happy. Not just happy to see me, but like this was a smile on top of happiness.

Her hair, by the way, was a deep auburn with teal highlights.

Teal.

Oh man.

I gave her a hug, even though it felt a little weird to hug Mom in front of my friends. When I introduced her to everyone, Sage threw her arms around Mom in a giant hug. Sage didn't feel awkward about hugging.

"An art fest?" Mom said, looking across the street. "Well, it looks like I came on the right day."

Eventually Mr. Wirtz found a parking space and joined us. That was weirder. I mean I knew him, but when you know somebody only as one thing, then you have to interact with them as something else, it just feels funny. He had been my teacher. Now he was Mom's boyfriend.

He adjusted his glasses, shook each of our hands in turn and said, "A pleasure to meet you."

I'd forgotten how he could be a little formal. Not in a weird way. More like in a way that felt like he didn't think we were little kids.

There was an awkward pause, broken by Mr. Wirtz.

"You know, on the car ride over, Laura and I were talking about how similar squirrels and cigarettes are," he said.

"What?" I said.

"Think about it," he said, his face serious. "If you stick either one in your mouth and start it on fire, it'll kill you."

All of us busted out laughing, even me.

"You can't get over that one, can you," Mom said, to Mr. Wirtz who was laughing as hard as any of us.

When the laughter died down, I took a deep breath. "Now for the big event," I said, mostly to my friends. "Taking them up to Dad and Dad-to-be."

Mom and Mr. Wirtz followed me up the stairs. Michael was writing new name plates for my recently invited guests. Dad was sliding them into the little frames as Michael finished each one. Something about watching Dad's huge hands work with those little frames was funny.

They both dropped what they were doing as we entered.

They made introductions all around. Mr. Wirtz shook Dad's and Michael's hands with a huge smile on his face. Mom did that double cheek kiss like people from Europe do.

Michael started pouring kombucha for

everyone.

"You want a glass, Jer?" he asked.

I shook my head. "So many parental figures all in the same room," I said. "I think I need to step out for some air."

They laughed.

When I left the apartment, I took a deep breath.

Mom was here.

When I was younger, I used to hope that one day Mom and Dad would get back together. But now that I was old enough to get it, I could see them apart and be happy for them that they'd moved on.

Maybe it was like how it used to be just Sage and I. But now it was actually better with more.

CHAPTER

"What's good to eat around here?" Mom asked. "We could take you somewhere and you could eat all the meat and sugar you want."

"So, like, McDonald's?" I said.

Mom and Mr. Wirtz laughed.

"Whatever sounds good to you," Mr. Wirtz said.

I thought for a minute. "I know exactly where to take you."

When we got to The Global Market, I led the way, pointing to highlights Asad showed me and other places we'd discovered. "Here's where you can get the best lamb in the world. And the epic tamales are just over there. Turkish food just around the corner. A sushi bar. If you try the cheese shop, stay away from the one called Gorgonzola."

We picked food from different places to make ourselves a sort of global buffet. Mr. Wirtz picked an eggplant curry. Mom got corn mushroom tacos. I got a rice bowl topped with the world's best lamb. We found a table and started eating. The food wasn't stuff I'd normally think to pick, but all of it was bold and bright.

When I slowed down a little, I looked over the table at Mom and Mr. Wirtz, digging their forks together to fight over a piece of eggplant. It was kinda weird. It was like they were on a date. But at the same time, I knew I was kinda on a date to see whether Mr. Wirtz and I could fall in love. So to speak.

I already liked him, but man. Did I mention the fact that I was getting tired of being the third wheel everywhere I went?

"Hey Jer," Mr. Wirtz said, finally surrendering the piece of eggplant. "Why did the bird fall out of the tree?"

"Why?" I asked, spearing another piece of lamb.

He shook his head sadly. "It was dead."

I just looked at him.

Mom shook her head. "I had to survive all these jokes once. Wasn't that enough?" she said. But she was twinkling at him.

"Why did the squirrel fall out of the tree?" he asked.

I shrugged. "Because it was dead?"

"No. Because it was stapled to the bird."

A laugh escaped me.

"And the raccoon? Why did he fall?"

"I have no idea," I said.

"Peer pressure."

Okay, that was actually pretty funny.

When we'd finally finished our feast, Mom and Mr. Wirtz leaned into their chairs across from me. Mr. Wirtz's arm hung over Mom's shoulder. It was so relaxed-looking, but so surprising I had a hard time not staring at it.

A silence settled over the table. The kind that a full stomach brings. Eventually, though, I thought maybe I should try to say something to Mr. Wirtz. He had told me all those jokes. I had really learned that any kind of relationship is what Mom calls a two-way street: both people have to try.

"So," I said. "How is Lila doing, Mr. Wirtz?"

Mr. Wirtz shook his head. "Please, call me Zeb."

That was gonna feel weird, but I could handle it at this point. "Not Zebulon?" I asked with a grin.

"Oh, lord," he said. "Definitely not." Zeb told

me about Lila. How she was starting ballet.

"Isn't she young for that?" I asked.

Zeb laughed. "It's more tripping around in tutus than dancing."

"But she's adorable," Mom said.

I felt a pang of stupid jealousy, but I pushed it aside.

"Hey Zeb," I said. "What has four legs, is green and fuzzy, and will kill you if it falls on you out of a tree?"

Zeb thought for a long time. "I give up."

I looked at him sideways."A pool table."

Zeb busted up laughing, and so did Mom. I laughed along with them.

It had taken me a long time to get used to sharing Dad with Michael. Now it looked like I was going to have to go through that process all over again.

At least this time I had experience.

After we cleared away our paper plates and compostable plastic forks, I told them, "I've got another place to take you."

"Where?" Mom asked.

"Paradise," I said. I led them to Bulshada.

Asad's dad greeted us loudly. "Doncha wanna wanta Fanta?"

"How about three teas?" I said. "And three halwas."

"Good choice," he said.

When we settled down with our tea and halwa, I started with a sip of the tea. It was spicy. Almost like Christmas.

Mom took a bite of the halwa. She closed her eyes and chewed slowly. When she finished, she looked at me and said, "You're a jerk."

"What?" I said. "Why?"

She smiled. "Because every dessert is going to be a disappointment after this."

We all laughed.

We nibbled our halwa and sipped our tea.

"This is perfect," Zeb said.

"Paradise," Mom said.

I swallowed another sip of tea. "Yeah," I said. "It is."

CHAPTER 31

The night before the wedding, Robi and Em came to pick up Michael who said it was bad luck to see each other before the ceremony on the wedding day. It seemed strange to me to have such an old-fashioned idea at such a modern wedding.

All of us loaded the tote boxes and doily

things in the back of Robi's SUV. When we went back upstairs the apartment felt clear. Like it could breathe again.

Dad got everyone something to drink while Michael started talking details with Robi and Em. The two of them were the masters of ceremony for the wedding. Robi was even the one officiating. Michael had compiled a three-ring binder of lists, contact info for each guest, every contact at their venue in Powderhorn Park, a copy of the vows. And on and on and on. Em said Michael's only job was to show up to the wedding and enjoy it. They would take care of the rest.

I had a hard time believing Michael could surrender that much control. But when he handed over the binder, his shoulders relaxed a little and he let out a sigh.

"Leave it to us," Em said.

"Okay," Michael said. "But I'm making us read through the entire binder before we go to bed tonight."

Robi and Em laughed.

"That's what slumber parties are for," Em said. "Plus manis, pedis, and facials."

Michael grabbed his bag. He and Dad hugged.

"I'll see you outside at the altar," Dad said. "By the lake. Until then."

They kissed. "Until then," Michael said.

They gave each other a look that was so sappy I was pretty sure it could've been boiled into syrup.

"No bachelor party for you, Dad," I said while we sat down with a bowl of popcorn to watch TV. "Or manis, pedis, or facials," I added.

"Nothing beats hanging out with you," Dad said, putting an arm around me.

I know that's the type of thing parents are supposed to say, but still, it can feel pretty great when they do.

During the night I woke to the sound of lightning and rain beating against the window.

No!

No rain.

Not allowed.

But I figured that if the rain started in the night, it would rain itself out by tomorrow. What was that thing Mom always said? Rain before seven stops by eleven. I could only hope.

But in the morning, the rain hadn't let up. It mostly fluctuated between drizzle and downpour. Dad was looking at the weather radar on his phone. "Not looking too good," he said. "It's looking like the ceremony will be in the pavilion."

"Michael is gonna be bummed," I said.

Dad set his phone back onto the table. "That's putting it lightly."

Dad and I dug umbrellas out of the closet and went out for coffee and bagels. Then we went to an old-fashioned barber shop on Lake Street. He said we were getting hot shaves. I had never shaved before. I had been saving the first shave for a special occasion. I figured a wedding was special enough.

We sat side by side in leather chairs. The barber was named Farzad. He tied those crinkly haircutting poncho capes around our shoulders.

He started with Dad, wrapping Dad's face in a hot towel that was fragrant with some kind of oil. After letting him steam for a few minutes, Farzad removed the towel, rubbed Dad's stubble with oil, brushed it with a thick, creamy lather and shaved until Dad's face was smooth and pink.

"Gorgeous," I told Dad. He and Farzad laughed, but I could see Dad's eyes were just a little distracted.

"What?" I asked as Farzad prepared a towel for me.

Dad sighed. "The rain."

"I don't know what the big deal is," I said. "It's just water. It's not like we'll melt or anything. And you've got the pavilion."

"Yeah," Dad said absently.

I got the hot towel at that point. It was just hot enough to feel hot without burning. It felt like my skin was opening up.

"I'd better check in on Michael," Dad said. "You'll have to pardon me for a minute."

I heard him get up and walk out the front door.

"If he leaves, you will have to pay, friend." Farzad laughed.

Dad came back by the time Farzard removed the towel. Farzad brushed my whole face with the creamy lather, not just my upper lip. He gave me a full shave. When he was done, I looked at the mirror at my fresh, smooth skin. No peach fuzz. No upper lip shadow. Somehow the lack of shadow-mustache made me feel older.

Dad was smiling at me. "You ready?"

"Yeah," I said. "You?"

He scratched behind his ear. "I don't think I've ever been readier."

As Farzad untied the poncho thing from around my neck, I got an idea. "Dude," I said. "Ponchos."

"Ponchos?" Dad said.

"Ponchos," I repeated. "For the wedding."

"Where are we going to get 100 ponchos?" Dad asked.

The wheels in my head were turning. "I know where we can get a gazillion," I said. "Two gazillion actually. I'm gonna have to make a phone call."

I stepped outside under the awning that sheltered me from the rain. I pulled out my cell phone. I pulled up Sage's number and typed *HELP!*

CHAPTER 32

When we got to the lakeside pavilion in Powderhorn Park, Dad opened his umbrella out the truck door. "Well," he said, "Let's swim on in."

He jumped out, slammed his door and ran around to my side. The two of us darted down the hill towards the building that stood near the lake. I was thankful that we hadn't taken our tuxes out of their now-soaked garment bags.

Inside, the hall looked perfect. Fresh flowers filled each of the teal canning jars. There was a perfectly tied stack of soap at each place next to the handwritten name plates. A multilayer canapé tray covered with little tarts and cheese-topped crackers stood on every table. Teal and chocolate napkins were rolled inside matching hand-painted napkin rings. The empty picture frames leaned against the wall near the line of tables that would become the food line. Edison bulbs hung from the ceiling surrounded by the doily globes, casting lacy shadows over the room.

Robi was already there in a long black skirt with a tuxedo shirt, jacket, and bow tie. They looked awesome.

Robi gave Dad a hug. "Congratulations!"

Em rushed over, and pulled Dad into a hug. Dad returned the hug, then pulled back and asked, "Are they here?"

I assumed that he meant Michael, but then realized he meant the Bridge van. And with it, the two blue garbage bags of our solution.

"On their way," she said. "I've been in touch with Lisa. Her number was listed in the comprehensive guest section of the wedding binder."

"What would we do without you?" Dad asked. "And Michael?"

"On his way," Robi said.

"Alright," Dad said. "Now, where do I get changed?"

Em laughed. "Do you want the bridal room or groom's room? Heteronormativity."

"I guess I should be traditional and choose bridal. I'm an old-fashioned queer."

Robi nodded. "I'll send Michael to the groom's room, then."

I followed Dad to the bridal room. It was bright white with tall mirrors, and hair dryers, curling irons on a long vanity.

Dad and I put on our tuxes. It was the first

time I'd worn a tux. I actually liked how I looked and felt in it. It was nothing like those stupid scratchy suits I'd had to wear when I was a kid going to church on Easter.

It was strange to see Dad so fancy. If fancy was the right word. Perfectly smooth shaven. His hair combed back off his forehead.

We heard a knock on the door and it opened just a crack.

"Is it safe?" came the voice of Mom.

"Get in here," Dad called.

Mom wore a long teal dress in exactly the shade of our bow ties. She could've been a bridesmaid.

"Look at you," she said. I thought she was talking to me, but her eyes were on Dad. "Brings back some memories," she said. Then she started laughing. "Aren't you glad we got ours over with?"

"You better believe it," Dad said.

She stood on tiptoes and kissed Dad on the cheek. "May your new marriage succeed in every way that ours failed."

"Hey," I said. "No kissing the bride yet."

They both laughed.

"Are you sure you don't want me to walk you down the aisle?" Mom said. "I gave you away once. I'll gladly do it again."

Dad laughed. "Thanks, but not in a hundred years. You're lucky to have a seat." He winked at her.

Mom punched his shoulder.

"Hey," Dad said. "I'm gonna need that later."

"Joy," Mom said, pulling Dad into another hug. "Joy to you." She left the room.

Soon, Em poked her head in the door. "They're here! The delivery has arrived."

I ran out into the reception room. It was filling up with people in shirts, ties, and dresses. People I knew and didn't know yet. Everyone from Cocktail Hour. Several people I recognized from Real Foods. And the barrage of faces from Michael's photo album.

But it was the group at the doors I was excited

to see. It was everyone from the Bridge van. Mustafa, Marner Saw, Ifaa, Nur, and Asli. Plus, Asad, Asha, and their parents. At the head of the group, Sage, Reina, and Lisa. Sage carried one of those blue garbage bags with ponchos spilling out the top.

"We called everyone," Sage said. "When we told them what you needed, they were all happy to loan back their ponchos."

"Thank you," I said to the group. "Thank you so much."

As I turned to bring the bag to Em, Asli called out to me, "*Who* are you?"

"Good," I said with a laugh. "No. I am great."

Dad sent me to get Michael. I found him in the groom's room. He stood with his arms out while his sister brushed him with a lint roller.

"Why your father took the room with the floor to ceiling mirrors is beyond me," he said with a laugh. "God knows he's not going to use them."

"He wants to talk to you," I said.

"We can't see each other before the ceremony. It's bad luck," Michael said.

I held up one of the large teal catering napkins. "He sent this. He's wearing one right now."

Michael glared at me like there was no way on earth he was about to tie this thing around his head, but then he shrugged. "This had better be good."

I helped him tie it around his head, over his eyes. I led him out of the room to where Dad stood waiting behind his blindfold. I guided Michael forward until the two of them found each other. Dad pulled Michael into a hug.

And all of a sudden Michael was crying. His eyes were covered, but I could hear it.

"What happened," Dad said. "Did I step on you?"

Michael hiccuped and gave a little laugh. "I'm just so happy this is finally happening," he said. "And just so..."

"What?" Dad said. "The rain?"

"Rain," Michael said. "Why? Why? Why? An outdoor ceremony. It was the one thing I really wanted. Tradition. My grandparents. My parents. Lake Superior. The Saint Croix. Under the open sky. But no. An outdoor wedding is *not* the one thing I want. The one thing is you." He sniffed and pulled back with a little smile. "But you better believe that an outdoor ceremony was a close second."

Dad laughed. "You really wanted that outdoor wedding, huh?"

"You know that." Michael buried his face into Dad's shoulder.

"Today we make our dreams come true," Dad said. "Ponchos."

"Ponchos?" Michael said.

"Ponchos," Dad repeated.

CHAPTER

It was funny to be all dressed up, wearing a tuxedo under a wrinkled up teal poncho. Well, it wasn't teal as much as grass green, but it was the closest to teal I could find in the mass of ponchos. Heather had bought two clear ones for Dad and Michael so you could see their tuxes underneath. Their ponchos at least had little creases all over them from being folded rather than the bunchy wrinkles that textured the rest of the ponchos.

The rain came down in sheets. It made the Powderhorn Lake look curtained with silver. I held the hood of my own poncho out from my head so the rain wouldn't run down my face.

I walked towards Robi in the spot between the willows that Michael had chosen. I was kinda both the ring bearer and also the best man. Being next to a lake at the bottom of a hill, the ground had turned marshy. Everyone clustered to two sides, making an aisle between them, but nobody was split between which groom they were there to support.

After I walked down the swampy aisle, Robi gave me a wink from under the hood of their poncho.

I looked at everyone. All sorts of new relatives that I knew I would have to meet later from Michael's side. Sage, Asha, Asad, Reina, Lisa, Asad and Asha's parents. Then Mustafa, Ifaa,

Asli, Nur, Marner Saw. I gave a little wave; they waved back at me, beaming. Everyone from cocktail hour. Mom and Mr. Wirtz. Or Zeb, I guess. Mom had pulled off her heels and gone barefoot, the wet grass squelching between her toes. I saw that she wasn't the only one who had abandoned their heels.

I looked out over all the ponchos: blue and white and orange and green and yellow and red. Together, they looked like a garden. Like the one behind Bridge.

Dad appeared out of the downpour in his clear poncho, carrying an umbrella over his uncovered head. He walked down the "aisle" and stood next to me and Robi. It was weird having a wedding without music. I guess the cellist they'd hired didn't feel like braving the elements.

"Ponchos," Dad laughed. He gave me a high five.

Then came Michael. And even though he was in a poncho and under an umbrella, his face was soaking wet. I looked up at Dad's and saw that his was, too.

Robi took a deep breath and started, their voice raised over the sound of the rain. "Dearly beloved, family of origin, family of choice, we gather here to celebrate."

After the ceremony, everyone rushed inside and piled the streaming ponchos into a wet mound by the guest book. It made the reception hall smell like plastic, but that didn't matter. I worked my way through the line of people taking turns hugging and kissing Dad and Michael. I finally found Asad, Asha, and their parents.

Their dad looked at me, his eyebrows raised. "Father marries father?" He threw up his hands. "America. Home of the brave."

Sage had come up right then just in time to hear what he'd said. Asha, Asad, Sage, and I looked at each other, then burst out laughing.

"They did it," Sage said.

"They did it," I said back. "Thanks for

gathering all the ponchos."

"Of course," Sage said. "That's what family's for."

Later, while shifting into place for a photo between Dad and Michael, I looked over the faces and people filling the pavilion. Sage introducing Marner Saw, Nur, and Asli to Big Ben and Little Jon. Asad and Asha drinking punch with their parents and two of Michael's cousins. Ifaa and Mustafa sipping coffee with Lisa and Reina. Heather handing a crying Gordon over to Em. Michael's Mom, three sisters, my new step aunts, uncles, cousins, and grandma. And all those other faces and names I was supposed to remember from Michael's family tree photo book.

But our family was nothing like a tree. No single trunk held us. That wasn't what my family was like.

Seeing all my friends from Bridge made me think about the garden again. About all those different plants surviving and coming back. I remembered what Robi said about companion planting, how the plants needed each other in order to thrive. The ones that weren't much on their own, but were everything together.

We nourished each other.

It's what we did.

It's who we were.

When the photographer told us to say cheese, I didn't have to. I was already smiling the biggest smile ever.

ACKNOWLEDGMENTS

It takes a community to publish a book. Thank you to all who helped bring this story to life.

To my partner, Kris: you listened to my ramblings, offered sage guidance, and had the patience and love to spur countless discussions on the title. Thank you.

Thank you to the incredible students from around the world who welcomed me as a volunteer in their classrooms.

Many thanks to my friends who took the time to read and offer advice and encouragement. And especially to Abbie and Kris with their enthusiastic willingness to sit down with a glass of wine and dream how to enrich the story.

Abundant gratitude to Rachel Joy for her perdurable collaboration finding the right words and figuring out ways to unlock the details.

Thank you to my agent, Stephen Fraser, for being my stalwart champion.

Deepest thanks to Keith Garton and the rest of the wonderful team at One Elm Books for welcoming and believing in this story.

And to Fian Arroyo for once again bringing the characters to life.